BONKERS Short Stories
VOLUME THREE

MIX-UP MAYHEM

First published in 2022 by Write Laugh
12 King Street, Rotorua, 3010, New Zealand

Text © Tom E. Moffatt, 2022

Illustrations © Paul Beavis, 2022

www.tomemoffatt.com

ISBN 978-1-99-116170-3 (print)
ISBN 978-1-99-116171-0 (ebook)

A catalogue record for this book is available from the National Library of New Zealand.

Cover design and illustrations: Paul Beavis
Developmental and copy editing: Anna Bowles
Proofreading: Marj Griffiths, Rainbow Resolutions
Proofreading and editing: Vicki Arnott, Story Polisher
Print book and ebook design: Write Laugh

MIX-UP MAYHEM

Written by Tom E. Moffatt

Illustrations by Paul Beavis

For Hazel, my wonderfully nutty number three.

BONKERS Short Stories
VOLUME THREE

"Strange how you couldn't sleep last night," Mum says, as I grab a breakfast bowl from the cupboard.

What's she on about?

"But I could sleep," I say, plucking a spoon from the drawer and joining her at the breakfast bar. "I slept really well."

I don't think I stirred once. I woke up in exactly the same position as when I fell asleep. Even so, I yawn as I fill the bowl with Coco Pops.

Mum watches me pour the milk in, her eyebrows on a slant. "But you told me you couldn't sleep. That's why you borrowed one of Dad's books."

I stare at her. She hasn't brushed her hair yet and little strands are poking out from her head like tiny wires. Maybe they're trying to escape because they realise she's going bonkers.

I turn my attention back to my breakfast. The milk has turned murky brown. I've been stirring the Coco Pops rather than putting any in my mouth. I'm just not that hungry today.

Mum looks at the muddy puddle of food in front of me. "I told you you'd spoil your appetite!"

"When did you tell me that?" I swear Mum is actually losing her marbles.

"In the middle of the night," she says, looking at me like I'm the one who needs to send out a marble search party. "When you poured yourself a second bowl of muesli."

There's no way that's true. I hate muesli! It's like cardboard shavings covered with dead flies. You wouldn't catch me eating two mouthfuls, let alone two whole servings.

Mum is clearly going bonkers. I rest my hands on my thighs and search her eyes for signs of madness. My finger finds a little lump stuck to my pyjamas. I pick it off and study it. It's a small grey flake that looks just like a bit of cardboard. Or could it be muesli?

Mum shakes her head slightly, picks up her coffee cup and takes it over to the sink.

What the heck is going on? I'm not the one who's losing it, am I?

Dad walks into the room with Ruby hanging off his neck like a human cape. "Here's my little super-reader!" he says, ruffling my hair like it's full of ants and he's doing me a favour. "I think it's amazing that you've taken what your teacher said on board. About needing to extend yourself in all areas, especially reading. Although *The Count of Monte Cristo* might be a bit tough for a first adult read."

I stare up at Dad, who has a pair of small hands wrapped around his throat like he's being strangled. He's looking down at me with a sideways smile and squinty eyes. He's actually proud of me. I can't remember the last time he looked at me that way.

I'm about to say, 'I don't know what you're talking about!' but I stop myself.

"Please may I be excused?" I say instead.

I spend the morning re-running the conversation in my head. According to Mum and Dad, I woke up in the middle of the night, had two bowls of muesli and read one of Dad's boring books. I've heard of sleepwalking, but sleepreading? And sleepeating-disgusting-breakfast-cereal? Either they're playing a trick on me or something very strange is going on. I have to get to the bottom of this.

Suddenly there's giggling all around me.

I yawn.

"Number fourteen!" says Mrs Harper, and the entire class giggles as one.

I realise I am in Maths. Mrs Harper has been harping on about something, but I was miles away.

I yawn again.

"Tim Hoffman, I think fifteen yawns in ten minutes might be a new school record."

I clench my jaws closed and manage to disguise number sixteen as a bit of a stretch.

"Were you up all night studying for tomorrow's maths test?"

"No, Miss," I say, but it comes out more like a groan.

Mrs Harper rolls her eyes and starts handing out practice papers. I don't stand a chance in Maths today. Things just aren't adding up.

"Why are you not playing football?" Armaan asks me as he polishes an apple on his trousers. It's lunchtime and I'm sitting on a bench in the playground watching a line of ants dismantle the crust of a jam sandwich. It's surprisingly relaxing.

"Too tired."

"You were up all night reading? I do that sometimes."

"No," I say, looking at him through my half-closed eyes. Then I think, what the heck, why don't I just tell him? Armaan is one of my best friends, after all. If I was a superhero, he'd be my sidekick. And he's pretty brainy. Maybe he can help me figure out what's going on.

"Here's the thing ... maybe I *was* reading all night. Mum says she saw me borrowing one of Dad's books and reading it in my room, but I don't remember any of it. And apparently I ate two bowls of muesli in the middle of the night too."

"Ooh, I love muesli!" says Armaan, then he takes a bite of his apple.

"I don't," I say. "It's disgusting."

"If you don't like it, why did you eat it?" Armaan asks, spraying little droplets of apple juice at me.

Here goes.

"That's the thing, I didn't. At least my mind didn't. I think my body did it without me knowing. Maybe someone borrowed it."

Armaan stares at me. I have no idea what he's thinking.

"My brother borrows my underpants sometimes. When I get them back they're all stretched and baggy."

Maybe this wasn't such a good idea. I'm now having a conversation about underpants with

Armaan. And not even the wear-on-the-outside superhero undies. The normal, baggy kind.

"Well, my brain feels stretched and baggy. And I know I didn't do all those things last night, so maybe someone else was using my body. What if there's an evil version of me that's trying to take over?"

Armaan takes another bite of his apple and chews it thoughtfully. "You think this might have happened before?"

That's a good question. I have been tired recently. Not always this bad, but certainly more than normal.

"Maybe," I say.

Armaan jiggles his head from side to side. "Someone could be borrowing it every night! You should set traps to see if your body gets out of bed."

I imagine waking up in the morning hanging from the ceiling by my ankles.

"What kind of traps?"

"In detective stories they put teeny bits of toilet paper in the bottom of doors," Armaan says.

"They wipe the door's bottom?" I ask, not really following what he is talking about. And what kinds of books does he read, anyway?

"No, you just place toilet paper against the doorframe and close the door. If it's fallen on the floor in the morning you know that the door has been opened." He looks up at the sky and his forehead wrinkles for a minute as though his brain is working in overdrive. Then he says, "Or you sprinkle chalk dust on the floor next to your bed and next day you see if you have chalky feet."

Those are actually good ideas. I spend the rest of my time at school trying to come up with other traps, but my brain is not cooperating.

That evening I nearly use my dinner as a pillow. The mashed potato looks so comfortable.

"Do you have any homework today, love?" Mum asks.

"Nyeoh," I say, hoping that they will hear what they want to hear. The truth is, I have no idea if I have any homework or not. I don't think I heard a single word my teacher said today. I must get some sleep.

When I get to my bedroom I try not to look at the bed. If I do, I'll fall asleep. I take the bit of toilet paper from my pyjama pocket, tear off a strip and wedge it between the door and frame. I also jam a piece in my top drawer, just in case.

It would be good to put a patch of chalk next to the bed, too, but who has chalk these days? And anyway, there isn't enough space between all the pieces of Lego and clothes scattered over the carpet.

Instead, I put my glass of water on the floor beside my bed. If you didn't know it was there, you would definitely knock it over. So if the carpet is wet in the morning I'll know my body was used by someone else.

Crawling into bed is the most enjoyable thing I have ever done in my life. My sheets are silky-smooth and my pillow is like a giant marshmallow.

Mum opens the door slightly and pokes her head in. "Night, dear," she says, and closes the door behind herself.

The little piece of tissue lying on the floor is the last thing I see before my eyes droop closed.

About three seconds later, Mum is perched on the end of my bed, shaking my shoulder gently.

"It's time to wake up, Tim," she says, "or you're going to be late for school."

I yawn as I look towards the curtains. How can it be light already? I only went to sleep a minute ago.

"Let me help you up," Mum says softly. Something weird is going on. Normally she'd be shouting at me from the kitchen, telling me to get my butt out of bed. "How's your foot feeling?"

I suddenly notice that my right foot is throbbing with pain, as though I've stepped in a fire.

"Your father and I are really proud of how you dealt with last night, love. You were so brave at the hospital. You barely even flinched when the doctor stitched you up. And I can't believe you were so adamant about still going to school today!"

Hospital? Stitched up? Adamant that I go to school?

As I pull my legs out from under the blankets, I glance at the floor to make sure I don't knock the glass of water over. But it isn't there.

Then I look at my right foot.

It's covered in an enormous bandage.

My jaw drops open. I have a pretty good idea what happened. I bet it has something to do with that glass.

Mum helps me hobble down the stairs to the kitchen where Dad is cutting toast into circles for Ruby. She won't eat it unless it's been cut into a random shape.

"It's the wounded soldier!" Dad says as I limp into the room, one arm wrapped around Mum's waist. "How are you feeling this morning?"

I let out a yawn that seems to go on for an entire minute. A bit of dribble spills from my mouth and drips onto my pyjamas, which are different to the ones I put on when I went to bed.

"Tired," I say, as I slump down into a chair.

"I'm not surprised," Dad says. "We were in A&E for nearly two hours. But don't worry, we won't force you to stay home today."

I stare at him blankly. This has to be some kind of joke.

By the time I get to school, I've attained a new level of tiredness. It reaches all the way up to my eyeballs, where it grabs my eyelids and pulls them down like a pair of blinds. Only the lower half of my eyes are still open, meaning that I can't see anything above waist height. My mouth is clamped shut and I'm making short raspy breaths through my nose.

Thinking is not an option. It's like my brain is deflating further with every out-breath. My back is arched and my shoulders hunched, since I don't have enough energy to keep them straight.

Must. Sleep. Soon.

As Mrs Harper hands out the maths tests, I let my eyelids slide shut, and my head lolls to the side. I know I shouldn't be doing this, but I can't help myself. The tiredness has ambushed me. I'm outwitted and outnumbered. Surrendering is my only option.

When I force my eyes open again, my vision is out of focus and I'm seeing double. The weirdest thing is that the test is over. In fact, the whole maths class is over. And everyone is getting ready for recess, which means that I missed English too. That can't be right. There's no way Mrs Harper would let me sleep through two lessons. Not in my wildest dreams.

Football wouldn't be an option today, even if I wanted to play. I hobble over to the same bench as yesterday and hope Armaan will join me. I need to tell him what I think about his idea of setting a trap.

"I can't believe you're so much better today," Armaan says, dragging his feet as he ambles over, a full five minutes after the start of playtime. "Even with your sore foot."

"You call this better?" I say, letting out a low groan. "I feel like I've had my brain removed."

"But you were the first to finish the maths test. And you answered more questions than me in English!"

"What?" I say, my eyes wide open for the first time all day. "I thought I slept through both lessons?"

"Oh no, totally the opposite," Armaan says, staring at me in awe. "You were quite brilliant."

"But that wasn't me, you idiot!" I say, not knowing where else to aim my anger. "That must have been Evil Tim."

"No, no, no," says Armaan, backing away slowly. "The other one was much nicer. You must be Evil Tim. I'm getting a teacher."

How can this be happening? Even my sidekick isn't on my side. But I can't let Armaan get away. He's the only one who can help me solve this mystery.

Armaan is walking quickly back towards the school building. At least, it's quick for Armaan. I could probably overtake him, even with my sore foot.

"Wait!" I call. "I'm sorry, Armaan. I didn't mean to snap at you."

He stops and turns to face me.

"Please," I say. "Tell me what I was like in Maths and English. I need to know what I'm up against."

Armaan strolls towards me, clearly not picking up on the urgency in my voice. "He was very polite. He said please and thank you. And he called Mrs Harper 'Madam'."

"And he did my maths test for me?"

"Yes, you were first to finish."

This makes no sense. My body can't possibly be getting taken over by someone nice. He's *taking over my body.* That makes him evil.

"What am I going to do to stop him?" I ask, my mind emptier than a poor man's pocket. "Even if he isn't evil, I can't have someone else using my body every time I doze off. And I'm not setting any more traps. The last one gave me this." I say, waving my bandaged foot in the air.

"Why don't you ask him what he wants?" Armaan says, scraping his shoe on the asphalt like he's trying to destroy a colony of ants. "He seemed like a nice guy. Perhaps he'll tell you why he's using your body."

I stare at Armaan, a smile forming on my lips. That's almost genius in its simplicity. In fact, I probably would have thought of it myself if I'd had some sleep and my brain didn't feel like a used tea bag.

I spend the rest of the school day doing everything I can to stay awake. Mrs Harper believes in a modern learning environment and lets us work wherever we like. That means we're allowed to sit on a beanbag all day, if we want. Obviously, that would not be a bright idea right now, so I spend all day balancing on one leg at one of the standing desks, which just about keeps me awake.

When I get home, I do my homework straight away for the first time ever. I'm serious, I do. But only because I know Mum and Dad will ask me about it at dinner time, and I don't want to have to do it later.

Through dinner I have to stifle seventeen yawns, but I don't think anyone except me is counting. When I eventually hobble to my room and get into my pyjamas, I feel like my brain is already asleep. I leave my school clothes scattered among all the toys and Lego bricks littering my floor.

I clear some space on my desk by shoving everything to the side and stacking a few comic books. Then I stare at a blank sheet of paper, trying to think what to write. I've had millions of questions popping into my brain all day, but right now only two come to the surface.

I write *Who are you?* and *What do you want?* in my most legible handwriting, then place the note on the chair, so it doesn't get lost among all the junk on my desk.

When I crawl into bed the clock says 18:47, which is a bit of a risk. What if Nice-Evil Tim gets up while my parents are still awake and makes himself at home? Well, it's too late to worry about that now. My head is already on the pillow and my eyes have closed for business.

Milliseconds later, beams of sunlight shoot through the window, trying to zap my eyeballs. I shield my face and sit up, carefully lowering my bad foot out of bed. The last thing I want to do is step on a piece of Lego or a *Star Wars* figure and send myself back to A&E.

The funny thing is, there are no toys on the floor. My room is completely spotless. A sheet of paper sits in the middle of my now-tidy desk. And it has writing on it.

This is it. I'm finally going to find out what's going on.

I hobble over to my desk as quickly as I can.

Underneath my own shaky handwriting is some beautiful joined-up script that was surely not produced by the same hand.

It says:

I'm Raymond Ainsworth.

I'd love a glass of Scotch, but the Body-Share Code of Conduct forbids it, so I'll settle for a cup of tea, if you're offering.

P.S. Sorry about the injured foot. I didn't see that glass on the floor. By way of apology – and further accident prevention – I decided to tidy your bedroom. I hope you don't mind.

I read his response several times, trying to get my head around it. What is the Body-Share Code of Conduct? Why is Raymond Ainsworth being told what he can or can't do in my body? It's *my* body. Shouldn't I be the one setting the rules?

Mum can't get over my tidy bedroom and it puts her in a fantastic mood. She makes me a stack of pancakes and even lets me pour my own maple syrup. Even after five pancakes there's still a sticky lake filling my plate. I'm not allowed to lick plates, so I use my thumb to mop it up and lick that instead.

Dad walks into the room with a newspaper tucked

under his arm. He seems pretty pleased about something, too.

"Here's my little chess player," he says, ruffling my hair again. "I can't believe you beat me, though. I'm going to call that beginner's luck. If you can't sleep again tonight, we'll have another match. I don't want you going too long thinking you can beat your old man at chess."

I smile in response and stifle another yawn. The tiredness is getting worse, not better. I lose count of how many times I yawn through breakfast. My mind is too busy trying to process what I've learnt.

What is a code of conduct, anyway? And why is Raymond so nice? Surely you'd have to be evil, or at least very selfish, to use someone else's body while they sleep.

After breakfast I get ready as quickly as I can and am standing by the door, ready to go, half an hour earlier than usual. Mum looks at me all squinty-eyed and puts her hand on my forehead to feel my temperature. But she doesn't say anything.

School is practically deserted when I get dropped off, so I wander around trying to find Armaan. He's always one of the first to arrive. I eventually find him in early morning brain-games club doing a crossword.

The teacher is engrossed in the newspaper and doesn't pay me any attention, so I pull out Raymond's note from my pocket and hand it to Armaan.

He bites his lower lip as he reads, as though he's still trying to solve a crossword clue.

"This is very interesting," he says, lowering the piece of paper.

I stare at him through my eye-slits, my brain too foggy to respond. I'm getting kidnapped every time I nap by a charming kidnapper, and Armaan finds it *interesting*.

"But what can I do?" I say, my eyes going all watery. "That stupid note tells me absolutely nothing. But I'm too tired to wait another whole day. I need to find out why this is happening. I can't go on like this. I just can't."

"Would you like me to ask Raymond why he's taking over your body?"

I stare back at him blankly.

"Yes," I say.

Why didn't I think of that? Actually, that's about the only question I know the answer to at the moment: Because my body hasn't slept in days and my brain has gone on holiday.

"Why don't you go to sleep there," Armaan says, pointing at a beanbag. "Once Raymond is here, I'll talk with him and find out what he wants."

Right now that seems like the best idea since the first caveman used his finger to pick his nose. I get to sleep and find out what's going on, both at the same time.

The beanbag scrunches all around me as I flop down and close my eyes. I expect sleep to swallow me immediately, but it doesn't come. It's like trying to sneeze on demand. My brain is whirring with questions that I want Armaan to ask Raymond.

"Find out how he's doing it," I say, my eyes still closed.

"And why he chose me."

"And make sure you tell him how tired I am all the time."

"And find out when he's going to stop."

34

"Just go to sleep, would you?" Armaan says, and I get the sense that he prefers Raymond to me, which gives me a gnawing feeling in my stomach. That doesn't help with my sleep at all, and I'm still lying there when the bell goes to signify the start of school.

I stand up and stretch as I let out an almighty yawn.

"Raymond?" says Armaan. "Is that you?"

"No," I groan. "I'm still me."

We hurry to class and sit down on the mat with the other kids. I choose the *My Little Pony* cushion, not as a fashion statement but because it is by far the comfiest in the room. A glance at the whiteboard tells me we have Maths first. Perfect.

Mrs Harper says, "In Maths today we are..." but that's all I hear.

The next thing I know, I'm in the cloakroom with my bag on my back and kids are filing out into the playground with their bags on their backs, too. As if it were home time.

Armaan turns to me with an enormous grin. "Do you have to go right now, or can we have another quick game of chess?"

"What?" I say. "You know I hate chess. It's so boring."

The smile slips from Armaan's face like ice cream sliding off a plate.

"Oh, Tim," he says. "You're back."

He doesn't look pleased about it.

We file out of the cloakroom and into the playground, where there are heaps of other kids milling around.

"Well?" I say, raising my eyebrows.

"Well what?"

"Did you talk to him? Did you find out what's going on?"

Armaan nods, and relief wafts over me like a warm breeze. Armaan says nothing, though.

Is he going to make me squeeze the juice out of him like a lemon?

"What did he say?"

"He said lots of things," Armaan says, the smile coming back. "He talked all day long. He's such an interesting man."

"Man?" I ask. "How old is he?"

"A hundred and two. That's why he decided to Life Share. His own body doesn't work very well any more. And he's nearly blind."

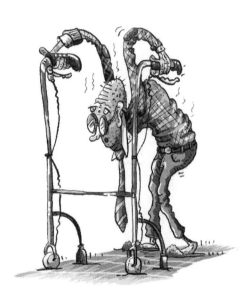

I stare back at him blankly as the words sink in. It's an old man whose own body is packing in. I guess that makes sense. At least, it explains why he's being so nice about it.

"Why is he coming into my body?" I ask. This is the million-dollar question.

"He doesn't know," Armaan says. I hadn't expected such a cheap answer. "He signed up to the Life Share Agency and they chose him a suitable body. He did say that he thought he was getting someone a bit older, but he loves being back in school. Oh, Raymond has a question for you..."

This conversation is not going how I expected it to go. How come he's asking me questions?

"What?"

"He wants to know if he could do another day shift tomorrow? Please say yes! We only had two games of chess. And he didn't finish telling me about the war."

Isn't it great when your best friend prefers hanging out with someone else? Someone ninety-two years older than you?

But on the bright side, it would mean that my mind would get some sleep. And I get to bunk off school while still being present. In fact, maybe I could use this to my advantage. I could do all the fun lessons and he could do all the boring ones.

"Okay," I say, nodding slowly as I think over what I've just learnt.

"Yay, thanks, Tim, you're the best." Armaan looks so happy that I consider changing my mind.

But I'm desperate to ask one more question, and the playground is thinning out now. I can see my mum over by the gate, chasing after Ruby.

"What's the Life Share Agency?" I ask.

"They specialise in finding host bodies for people who need them. Oh… you never told me how much money you're making!"

"Money?" I say, not looking towards Mum who is now waving at me. I'm not making any money. I only get one dollar pocket money a week. My parents give me ten cents per year of my age. My poor sister only gets forty cents a week.

Hang on a moment, though. If Raymond continues to share my body, my pocket money will have to go up. He's over a hundred years old!

"Raymond pays 999 dollars for an eight-hour day! He says more than half of that is going to you."

My jaw drops open, but I'm not able to respond. Mum has walked over with Ruby under one arm.

"Come on, please, Timothy," she says, her face set to impatient mode. "I need to get dinner on."

When we get home I tell Mum that I'd like to do my homework in my room, since it's nice and tidy. She totally buys it and even lets me use the laptop unsupervised. Which is another first.

As soon as my door is closed, I jump on the internet. I type 'Life Share Agency' into Google and there are thousands of hits. The first few are ads, so I skip down a bit and find what I'm looking for.

Their website is flashy. It says things like, 'Are you tired of your own body?' and 'Want to spend time in exotic parts of the world, but hate flying?'

I go to their contact page and they have offices all around the country. I find the closest one and jot the number down. My heart is beating surprisingly fast. This could be it. The moment I find out what is going on.

An automated voice answers the phone and gives me heaps of options. I've no idea which one to choose. Am I experiencing technical issues with my host body? Or do I need to discuss payment terms and conditions? In the end I select 'speak to an operator' and a bored-sounding lady answers the phone in monotone.

"Life Share Agency, how can I help you?"

"Hi," I say, not knowing where to start. "A man is sharing my body."

"Can I have your account number, please?"

"I don't have an account number. I didn't even know your company existed until someone started taking over my body every time I fell asleep."

"Okay," she says. "I'll just pop you through to the Unauthorised Visits department. Have a nice day."

The phone rings again and this time a man answers. I start over again.

"Hi, umm, someone is using my body when I go to sleep."

"Account number, please." This guy sounds bored too.

"I don't have an account number. I'd never even heard of your company."

"Name, please."

"Tim Hoffman."

"How do you spell that?"

"H-O-F-F-M-A-N"

"I'm sorry, sir, we don't have anyone by that name on our records."

"That's because I have never joined your company!" I say, a bit louder than intended.

"So how can I help you today, sir?"

"I want you to stop sending someone into my body every day!"

"Sorry, sir, but without a valid name or account number I can't help you."

A groan leaks out of my mouth. It doesn't help that I'm nearly falling asleep with the telephone as a pillow.

"Raymond!" I say, blurting the name out as it pops into my head. "The man's name is Raymond Ainsworth!"

The man types it in so loudly it sounds like he's attacking the keyboard with a pickaxe.

"Ah, yes. Tim..." the guy says eventually. "It says here that Raymond is scheduled to be with you for eight hours a day for the next six days."

I groan again.

"But why me? I didn't sign up for this."

"Yes, you did. Your signature is right here. Tim Hoffman. Wait a second, this says H-O-F-M-A-N-N."

"That's not me!" I say, unable to keep the excitement out of my voice. "I'm two Fs, one N."

"Okay, sir," the man says, his voice less animated than a dead dog. "I'll need you to fill out an incorrect assignment form on our website."

"Will that stop it from happening?"

"Yes, sir. All transmission will cease after five to ten working days."

My head thumps down on the desk.

"But can't you stop it now?" I say, in one long groan. I don't think I can survive another week of tiredness like this.

"I'm sorry, sir. Without termination requests from both parties, that is the best I can do. However, I've put a note in the records, so no further transmissions will be sent to your estate."

"So … umm … does that mean it's just going to stop?"

"Yes, sir. After this six-day excursion there will be no further visits."

"Okay," I say, glad to have finally got to the end of this exhausting conversation.

"Can I help you with anything else today, sir?"

"No."

"Thank you for using the Life Share Agency. You have a wonderful day."

I hang up and look around my tidy bedroom. Six days! How am I going to get through six more days without sleep?

Dinner is a painful experience. Ruby loves pasta. Not because she likes the taste, but because it sticks when she throws it at things. An hour later, when I'm getting into my pyjamas, I discover that I'm wearing a spaghetti necklace.

Before I climb into bed I sit at my desk and write a quick note for Raymond.

Hi Raymond,
Did you have a nice day at school today? I don't mind if you do Maths and English tomorrow, but we've got PE all afternoon and we are doing a mini football tournament. I've been looking forward to it for ages, so could I please take over at lunchtime?
Thanks,
Tim

When I wake up the next morning, the first thing I notice is a big puddle of dribble on my pillow. It's about the size of a small lake. I must have been in a pretty deep sleep for all of that to spill out of my mouth.

The second thing I notice is how amazing I feel. Seriously! It's like I've just slept for a fortnight. The clock says 07:22, so it's not even that late, but after not sleeping for a few days my body finally feels rested. And my foot doesn't hurt at all any more.

There's a note on my desk from Raymond.

Good morning, Tim,

I had a splendid time today, thanks for asking. This is such a great life that you've got. And Arnold is a wonderful friend. I regret that I am unable to spend any time in your company, since I am sure we would become friends too.

You may certainly have your body back at lunchtime and I hope you enjoy your football competition, but please go easy on that foot of yours.

Warmest regards,
Raymond

Things are actually looking great, all of a sudden. I don't have to do any of the boring bits at school any more. And I'm not even tired.

By the time I'm sitting down on the mat in class I am beginning to feel rather lucky. And that's before Mrs Harper hands out the maths test results!

"Tim Hoffman," she says, shaking her head and handing my test sheet to me. "If I hadn't seen you sit this test with my own eyes, I wouldn't believe it. Your handwriting is immaculate and you're the only person in the class who got top marks."

I look at the piece of paper, which has '20/20' written at the top and have to hide a smile. Perhaps this body mix-up is not so bad after all.

I barely feel tired at all until Mrs Harper begins the maths lesson, then my eyelids start to droop. I cover my eyes with my hand and try to make it look like I'm studying the test paper on my desk.

The next thing I know there are five or six kids piled on top of me. Arms are wrapped around me and they're saying things like "Great goal, Tim," and "That was epic!"

I pull myself free from the bundle and try not to look too annoyed. After all, I'm supposed to have just scored an epic goal. But I feel cheated. Raymond said he would let me have the football tournament.

It isn't long before the whistle blows for full time. My teammates cheer again and slap me on the shoulder and we walk from the pitch.

Armaan is waving at me from the side-line, so I head his way.

"Wow, that was great, Raymond," he says, his eyes as big as footballs. "You're a really good player!"

"It's me," I say, trying to keep the annoyance from my voice. "You know, Tim. The official owner of this body."

"Wow … that goal was incredible, Tim. Where did you learn to do that?"

"Okay, so that wasn't me. But it should have been. I thought the football tournament was on my shift?"

"That was my fault. Sorry." Armaan raises his shoulders and pulls a guilty grimace. "I told Raymond you wouldn't mind if he played the first game. I just wanted to see how good he was. He used to be the best footballer in his regiment."

I look up at the cloudy sky. Sharing a body is hard enough. But sharing friends is even more difficult. Everything Armaan says makes me think he likes Raymond more than me.

For the next two games my teammates keep looking over at me, as if waiting for a flash of brilliance. Then I get subbed off. We don't even make it to the semi-final.

"How was school today?" Mum asks on the way home.

"Good," I say, looking down at my muddy knees. I don't think she'd be too impressed if I said I didn't know. But it would have been more truthful. I have no idea what Raymond got up to for the day and we were so busy during football that Armaan didn't have time to fill me in.

The next morning I don't wake up until 07:45 and I feel like I've just emerged from hibernation. And there isn't even a note from Raymond.
Perhaps he feels

bad about taking the first football match without my permission.

The trouble is, it's hard to be annoyed at someone so nice. I decide to let him have the entire day at school today. He is really old, so it's great that he can have some time in a young body. And there's nothing too exciting going on, anyway. I tell Armaan my plan, then wait until after roll call and close my eyes. But I can't seem to fall asleep. My body's just not tired enough after such a great rest.

I'm so alert throughout Maths and English that I can actually follow what Mrs Harper is going on about, for a change. I even find our history lesson interesting.

The next thing I know it's the end of the day and Mrs Harper is telling us that we have another maths test and a spelling test tomorrow. Perfect. Raymond can take the whole day if he likes, to make up for today.

That night I write another letter and leave it on my desk.

Dear Raymond,

Sorry about today. I just wasn't able to fall asleep. And I really don't mind that you took the first football match yesterday. I just wish I could have seen your goal. Everyone said it was epic.

Feel free to take the whole day tomorrow. But when you are doing the tests, please can you make your handwriting a bit messier than normal so that it looks like mine?

I wish we could spend some time together too. I will write you a letter every day instead.

Have a great time at school,

Tim

P.S. My friend's name is Armaan, not Arnold.

When I wake up the next morning I leap out of bed and rush over to my desk to see what Raymond said. But there's no reply.

I quickly reread what I wrote to Raymond and realise that I didn't actually ask him a single question. Plus I feel completely refreshed. Perhaps Raymond didn't visit at all in the night, since he's now taking the day shifts.

When Maths begins, I cover my face with my hand and close my eyes. Nothing has happened by the time Mrs Harper hands out the test papers. It's okay, though. Raymond will be here soon.

The other kids start scribbling away, but I just wait patiently.

"Tim Hoffman!" Mrs Harper's voice startles me and I drop my pencil. "I hope you're not sleeping through a maths test?"

"No, Miss," I say, wiping a bit of drool from my chin. I look down at my test paper. It looks back at me blankly.

Very blankly, in fact. The only thing written on the answer sheet is my name.

If I stare at it hard enough, perhaps the questions will answer themselves.

Unfortunately, they do not.

When there are only five minutes left in the test, I read the first question. It's not actually as hard as I thought it would be, considering that I've barely been in any maths lessons for over a week.

I quickly answer the first few questions before our time runs out and Mrs Harper collects the papers. I swear she looks relieved when she sees my mostly blank sheet, as though it's just been proven that fairies don't exist.

As we get our reading books out Armaan looks over at me with an expectant smile.

I shake my head and his smile droops.

Where is Raymond? It isn't like him to be late.

I sleep through most of Reading and half of Literacy, but there's still no sign of him.

When Armaan and I sit at our usual bench at break time, it's hard to imagine that the day could get any worse.

"Maybe the Life Share Agency stopped sending him already?" I say, but as the words leave my lips, I realise that it's probably not true. And that the day could get a lot worse.

Armaan says what I don't want to say.

"Maybe he died."

We sit in silence for the rest of recess. I hope we're wrong but I can't come up with another likely explanation. Raymond was always so punctual and reliable.

At lunchtime we go to the library. Armaan gets on a computer and Googles the word *Obituaries*. It's not a word I've ever used before but I know exactly what it means.

That's when we see Raymond's obituary in the local newspaper:

Raymond Ainsworth - March 24th 1922 to May 8th 2024 - Passed away peacefully in his sleep after a long and happy life. Funeral will take place at St John's church at 1 p.m. on Saturday.

I look up at Armaan, who's gone all blurry. I quickly wipe my eyes. He doesn't say anything. He just keeps looking down at his shoes.

What is there to say?

Raymond isn't coming back. Which is what I wanted. But not like this. I know he was 102 years old. But we were just getting to know him. It's not fair.

The rest of the school day is blurry too. I fight the tears back until I get home and go up to my room. After all, what would I say I was crying about? Mum would never believe me. And if she did, she'd go nuclear.

When the tears do come, there are lots of them. My pillow is soaked in seconds.

I feel a bit better after that. Then I sit at my desk and reread all of Raymond's letters.

Mum drops me and Armaan off at the church on Saturday afternoon. We told our parents that Raymond had visited school and we'd got to know him there. Which is not entirely untrue.

I'm wearing my smartest trousers and a shirt. Armaan is in a black suit with a white flower pinned to his jacket. His hair is brushed to the side, making him look much smarter than me.

I've never been to a funeral before. I expected everyone to be crying. And wearing black. But it's not like that at all, maybe because Raymond was so old. People are standing around laughing and chatting. Some of them are dressed in black, but lots are not. Raymond's wife, Hilda, is wearing a bright pink dress and has a smile on her face. She looks more like she's at a wedding than her husband's funeral.

I stick close to Armaan. We're the youngest people here by about fifty years, maybe more.

There's a coffin at the front of the room. The lid is off and I can see a tuft of grey hair from here. Part of me wants to rush over to see what he looks like. Another part wants to run out the door. I've never seen a dead body before.

Hilda totters up to us, using a walking stick for support. "Are you here to pay your respects, my dears?"

We both nod. Armaan is looking paler than usual.

"Did you know my Raymond?" she asks.

Armaan nods more enthusiastically this time, a smile breaking out on his face. I nod too. Technically, I never met him. But we had a lot in common for a while.

Hilda's wrinkles change angles and she purses her lips in thought. Then she says, "You're not Tim and Arnold, are you?"

We both nod again and I say, "Yes," just to show her we're not mute.

A huge smile spreads across her face and her wrinkles multiply. "Raymond told me all about you two!" she says. "He was having such a wonderful time with you both. He honestly didn't want it to end."

"Neither did we," Armaan says, finding his voice.

"I don't suppose you ever met him in the flesh, did you?"

We shake our heads.

"Here, come along. I'll introduce you."

She shuffles over to the open casket, her walking stick thudding on the wooden floorboards. There's a large screen at the front of the church displaying photos of Raymond throughout his life. A black-and-white picture of him as a young man pops up. He's wearing an Eighteenth Battalion uniform. There's a knowing smile on his face and his kind eyes are staring straight at the camera.

I look down at the coffin.

Many years have passed, but behind the wrinkles and grey hair I can see the same man. A similar smile sits on his face, and although his eyes are closed, he still has a kind, friendly look about him.

I reach over and hold Armaan's hand. We stand like that for a few moments, looking down at Raymond's body.

The photos on the screen above us keep changing. A young Raymond on safari in Kenya. Raymond with his eldest daughter, Rita, on his shoulders. Raymond holding hands with his beautiful bride.

I wipe my eyes and look up at the old lady in the pink dress beside us. She's a wrinklier version of the lady in the photo. She smiles at me again and then totters off to talk to someone else.

Even though I never actually met Raymond, I feel like I know him so well. He looks peaceful, like he's sleeping. And I'm glad he was able to enjoy his last days in my body.

A photo of a football team pops up onto the screen. I can see Raymond's friendly smile on a player in the middle. He looks so happy that I suddenly feel bad about not letting him play in the football tournament. At least Armaan let him have one game.

Hang on.

I came back to my body with the players all piled on top of me. And that was the last time he was here. That means that one of his last actions in his 102 years of life was scoring an epic goal. How cool is that?

I look at the other players in the football photo. To the right of Raymond is another striker, Alfred Inglis. To his left, the goalkeeper, Hiko Eruera. As I look along the line of faces, I realise that I know all of their names. And which towns they're from.

How can I possibly know that?

I glance at the sign next to the coffin.

Raymond Edward Ainsworth - March 24th 1922 to May 8th 2024

May the eighth?

That was Wednesday. The day of the football tournament.

Armaan is looking at me, his eyebrows tilted in concern.

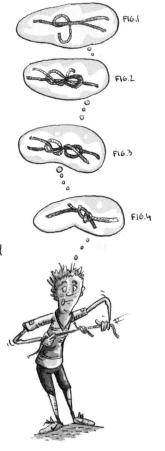

FIG.1

FIG.2

FIG.3

FIG.4

My shock must be showing in my face.

Raymond died while he was in my body. And now I seem to know many of the things he knew. Like how to tie a fisherman's knot or fix a head gasket.

I put my arm around Armaan for support and we stagger over to the closest row of seats, my mind spinning.

I think back to school yesterday. And the day before. The questions in that maths test weren't that hard. And I knew most of what Mrs Harper was going on about.

This is ... this is ... AMAZING! School is going to be a doddle.

A photo of Raymond playing chess pops up on the screen. A smile curls the edges of my lips as I look at Armaan.

"Once the service is over, maybe we should have a game of chess?" I say.

I've got a feeling I'm going to win.

It's funny the things you notice at significant moments in your life.

At the time of the accident, I spotted a dog peeing.

Seriously. I did.

I was staring out the car window, watching houses and trees swish by. Mum, Dad and Luke were still playing Monopoly on the car's central table. Luke had that smug expression on his face, the one he always gets when he's winning, so I was actually glad I'd gone out

67

of the game. It meant I didn't have to look at him any more. I could look out the window instead.

That was when I saw the dog. It had the same kind of walkie-bot that Savannah's family uses, and was pulling so hard on the leash that the droid's wheels slid along the grass. When the dog got close enough to the fence, it cocked its leg and peed against the corner post. As it peed, it did a funny squint, revealing a row of pointy white teeth. A streak of wee darkened the wood.

Movement further up the intersection caught my eye. A silver car was travelling quickly towards us. Too quickly. Its driver was looking over his shoulder, but no auto-drive computer would go that fast, so I could tell he had it in manual. If he'd seen the intersection, he would surely have slowed down. My eyes and mouth went wide, but I didn't have time to say anything.

I clamped my eyelids shut at the moment of impact. It was the loudest thing I'd ever heard. My whole world filled with the sound of glass smashing and metal twisting, all happening at once.

During the quiet that followed, there was groaning and shuffling, and then the steady beeping of the Life-Preservation Drones. They must have found us quickly.

I don't recall much after that. Just images ingrained in my memory.

Blood on my hands.

Mum crying.

Dad sprawled on his back with an LPD attached to his head.

And pain. I remember an awful lot of pain.

I also got my first look at an LPD up close. Its sleek metallic frame and whizzing blades filled my entire vision. Robotic arms reached out on either side of my head.

Then there was nothing.

The next thing I knew I was sitting on a hard plastic chair in a tiny cubicle, like one of those self-cleaning toilets we have by the school playground. My bum was numb and my body ached. But not injury aches. The kind of aches and pains you get after sports day. Or when you've lifted too many heavy things, like the time we moved house and Dad refused to hire any removal droids.

The doors hissed open, revealing Mum, a man in a lab coat holding a silver tablet, and a tall male clone. Mum had a clump of bandages on her forehead and her left arm was in a sling. But other than that, she didn't look too beaten up.

I turned my eyes to the clone. He had the usual shaved head and QR code on his forehead. But his piercing blue eyes were staring hard at me, and there was a sympathetic look on his face. It was Dad. It had to be. The clone was too old for Luke, and

I remembered seeing the Life Preservation Drone on Dad's body.

The man with the tablet leaned forwards and removed suction cups from each of my temples.

"Alison Greene?" he asked.

I nodded.

"Good."

Mum let out a puff of air and looked up at the sky.

"Please select your date of birth." He spun the tablet around, its screen displaying six different dates. I tapped the third one.

The device pinged and the screen said, "Verification complete."

"I need to inform you that you've been in an accident," the man went on. "Your body has sustained serious injuries and will be recovering for quite some time. In the meantime, you'll have full use of a young female loan-clone."

I lifted my hands up to examine them. The skin was paler than my own and the fingertips were hard and rough.

"Please move and bend all your limbs, one by one, then wiggle your digits. I need to know of any faults or injuries before you leave."

I bent my arms and wiggled my fingers, before moving on to my legs and toes.

"There's a twinge of pain in my left knee," I croaked, the words barely scraping their way out of my throat. "And my voice barely works," I added.

Mr Tablet looked down at his tablet. "The voice is completely normal. It just needs a little time to warm up. And the knee was reported by the last user. We've injected some nanobots into the area, so it should be fully repaired within a week or two."

"A week or two?" I squawked. "How long will I be in this body?"

"Like I said, your own body sustained some serious injuries. It won't be ready to inhabit for at least a month. Perhaps even two or three. You'll receive a full doctor's report via instant messaging."

I lifted my hand to my head to feel the fuzzy shaved hair and let out a groan. I couldn't believe I'd have to go to school in a clone's body. What would Savannah say? And the other girls? They were going to hate seeing me like this.

Mr Tablet stepped out of the way and Mum rushed in to give me a cuddle. Even through this new nose and with a clone's hands, my mother still smelt and felt the same. I was suddenly grateful for modern technology. Without the LPDs, I'd probably be dead. And so would Dad.

"I'm so glad you're okay," Mum said. She must have been thinking the same thing. "And don't worry. You'll be back in your own body in no time."

    I buried my face further into Mum's shoulder, soaking up her smell and the softness of her overalls. She flinched and I remembered her broken arm. When I pulled away, I saw the clone – or Dad – standing beside Mum awkwardly.

"I won't give you a cuddle, Ali," he said, his voice also sounding raspy and strange. "That would be a bit too weird right now."

"How's Luke?" I asked, half hoping he was in a loan-clone too. It would be easier going to school if we both had one.

"He's okay," Mum said. "Just a few bumps and scrapes. He's at home already. Auntie Kaz is looking after him."

Auntie Kaz isn't a real auntie. She and Mum have been friends for years. She's got a daughter my age, too, called Olivia. We were close when she was little, but since then she's become a bit annoying. She always hangs out on her own, reading books or playing those stupid dress-up SIMs. Savannah and the others can't stand her. I really hoped she wasn't at home, too.

The tablet man strolled off to deliver bad news to another poor clone, and we made our way to the car park. To my surprise, we walked up to our car. A red Fordomation.

"But didn't it..." I said, my voice trailing off.

"Oh, this is a replica," Clone-Dad said, pressing the palm of his hand against the window. The car beeped but didn't unlock. Dad looked down at his hand and shook his head. "The insurance company had it made yesterday. They copied the AI and all the settings over, but I'll need to re-programme it to work with my new fingerprints."

Mum casually placed her index finger on the window and the doors unlocked. It was weird being back in a car. Practically the same car.

The table was packed away now and Dad sat in the manual drive position, as though he no longer trusted the auto-drive. My stomach squirmed with nerves the whole way home. I kept getting flashbacks to the peeing dog and the silver car speeding towards us. Mum must have felt the same. She didn't let go of my hand until we pulled into our driveway.

When we got inside the house, Luke was sitting on the couch building towers with his Zbox. Tall holographic shapes filled the middle of the room. And Olivia filled my favourite armchair.

I forced a smile.

Olivia looked up at me and grinned, looking deep into my eyes. If she felt any discomfort about my new body, she didn't show it.

Luke, on the other hand, glanced up and curled his lip in disgust. "Ouch! I can't believe you've got to go to school like that! It's gonna be a nightmare."

Mum glared at Luke. "One more comment from you and I'll confiscate your Zbox for the entire time Alison is in that body."

"Calm down," Luke said, focusing his attention back on his holographic blocks. "I'm just saying it how it is."

"I think it's great you got a clone that's around our age," Olivia said, still smiling at me as though nothing had changed. "When my cousin had to use one, they'd run out of kid clones, so he spent six weeks in an adult body. That would have been way worse."

I looked at Olivia and tried to force the edges of my mouth into a smile. Her hair was a bit shorter than it had been when I last saw her.

But other than that, she looked as geeky as normal. She was at least a foot taller than all the other girls at school and her long legs poked out awkwardly from a pair of denim shorts. She had the usual heavy black shoes on her feet, which Savannah said made her look like a golf club.

Before I could say anything, Auntie Kaz entered the room and rushed over to give me a cuddle. Her perfume was much stronger than Mum's but it smelt nice. Like a sweet fruit cocktail. I held the cuddle for as long as I could. Tears were welling up in my eyes and I didn't want the others to see.

Luke was right about one thing. School was going to be a nightmare.

The next morning the doorbell went while I was sitting in my bedroom, looking in the mirror. Instead of my curly blonde hair and blue eyes, I was staring at the clone's pale face and shaved head. The eyes were puffy from crying, which made me look even worse. And my school uniform looked simply ridiculous. They might have got the age right, but this body was much taller than my own and none of my clothes fitted. The sleeves of my school blouse ended halfway between my elbows and wrists.

As I fought back another wave of tears there was a gentle knock on my bedroom door.

"Who is it?" I tried wiping my eyes on my sleeve, but mostly got bare skin.

"It's me. Olivia."

Great. That was just what I needed. She was probably here to walk to school with me. I'd get teased not just for being stuck in a clone's body for three months, but also for hanging out with a geek.

I opened the door.

Olivia was standing there, all sheepish, with a large plastic bag dangling from her wrist. She now had three pink hair clips in her new hairdo. I mean, seriously? Did she think she was still six years old?

"I thought you might need this," she said, looking me up and down while she held out the plastic bag.

I took it from her and peered inside.

Clothes, all ironed and neatly folded. Right on top was a school uniform.

"I thought some of my stuff might fit you better than your own clothes," she said, looking down at her feet. "There are also a couple of pairs of shoes by the front door."

"Oh. Thanks, Olivia," I said. "That's really sweet of you."

And it was. It was a very kind thing to do.

Except, what would my friends say if they saw me wearing Olivia's clothes? They'd think it was the funniest thing they'd ever seen.

Especially if I had to wear a pair of her clumsy black shoes.

I reached in and grabbed the school uniform from the top of the pile. That would definitely come in handy. And perhaps I could wear some of the other stuff until I could get to the shopping centre to buy some decent clothes.

"I'm just going to put this on now, if that's all right?" I said, holding the school uniform up.

Olivia looked at my exposed wrist and smiled. "I think that might be a good idea."

She backed away as I closed my bedroom door.

By the time I left my room a few minutes later, I was feeling much better. Olivia's school uniform actually fitted well and I felt almost normal.

When I entered the kitchen, Dad's clone was making a cup of tea and Mum was sitting down at the counter, reading the newspaper.

"Where's Olivia?" I asked, surprised that she wasn't loitering about.

"She's gone to school already," Mum said, looking up at me and smiling. "She thought you'd probably want to walk in on your own."

"Oh, okay," I said. That wasn't what I'd expected, but would certainly make my entrance a lot less painful. And let's face it, it was already going to be painful enough.

"It was very nice of her to bring you some clothes," Dad said, plopping himself down next to Mum.

"Yeah, it was," I said, as I walked towards the door to see what shoes she had left me. There was no way I would wear a pair of her 'golf club' shoes. I'd rather go barefoot.

Amazingly, they weren't that bad. They were feminine, without too many frilly bits. And they fit my clone's feet just right. Why the heck didn't Olivia wear these, rather than the ugly things she usually had on her feet?

I had to admit it, I owed Olivia one. Big time.

Mum got all teary when I went to leave the house.

"Are you sure you're going to be all right?"

"Yes, Mum. I'll be fine." I think it sounded like I meant it. I held her gaze, then leaned in and gave her a quick cuddle, so she wouldn't worry. Because I was doing enough of that for the both of us.

The moment I stepped out the front door I knew that all my worrying had been justified. Everyone on the street turned to look at me. Little kids pointed until their mums and dads told them off.

Older kids laughed and said things like, "Ooh! Another kid has got a cloaner. Unlucky!" Or "I'm glad I don't have to go to school like that!"

By the time I got to the school gate, my throat was so tight it felt like the oxygen couldn't get into this stupid body. Everyone, and I mean everyone, was looking at me. It was like being an alien with six heads.

I stepped into the playground to a wave of hushed whispers. Alfie, a boy in my class, walked straight up to me.

"Is that you, Alison?"

I nodded.

"I heard what happened. What a bummer!"

I nodded again, glancing round the playground. I could see Luke over on the field chatting to a group of mates. He must have been the only person there who wasn't looking at me.

My breathing was so fast I was practically panting like a dog. Where the heck was Savannah? Or Mikaela? Or any of the others?

Of course, I could see Olivia sitting on a bench on her own with a book in her hand. She gave a half-smile and a half-wave, and for a second I was tempted to walk over to her. It was better than standing there on my own.

Then I saw Savannah's gorgeous red hair at the other end of the playground and I let out a huge sigh of relief. She was just stepping out of the office, Mikaela and Grace by her side.

She was smiling and chatting happily until she looked up and saw me. Her eyes bulged and the smile fell from her face.

She headed towards me and I had to stop myself from breaking into a run.

"O.M.G!" Savannah said, once we were within range. "I can't believe you're in a clone! How does it feel?"

My relief was so strong I felt lightheaded and it took me a second to answer.

"Oh, you know, it's a bit weird."

Now that I'd found them, I suddenly felt self-conscious. The three of them were just so beautiful. Not a hair was out of place. Their uniforms were pristine. And there I was. A tall, pale clone with a shaved head wearing Olivia's school uniform. I didn't fit in at all.

"I can't believe it's you in there, Ali," Mikaela said. "You poor thing."

"I know, right?" Grace said, stroking a lock of her gorgeous dark hair. "That's my worst nightmare."

"How long are you going to be like that?" Savannah asked, pressing her lips together as she gestured to my body.

"I don't know. A few weeks," I said, playing it down as much as I could. "Maybe a month."

"A whole month? You've gotta be kidding!"

The three of them stood there shaking their heads, as though wondering how *they* were going to cope. I was glad when the bell rang and everyone headed towards class.

Mrs Imani rushed over the moment she saw me, her arms stretched out wide. "Alison, you poor little dear."

She pulled me into her large frame and held me in a tight cuddle. It was actually the best I'd felt since arriving at school.

"How are you coping with the adjustment?" she asked, whispering directly into my ear. "It can take a few days to settle in."

"I'm okay, I guess," I said, surprised that the words made it past the lump in my throat. "Although, I don't feel quite myself."

"That's understandable. But it's still you in there, which is what matters. The outside is just for other people to deal with." She gave me a squeeze to signify the cuddle was over. "They'll get used to it soon enough. And if they can't, then they're not worth worrying about."

Once I was sat at my usual desk with my usual pencil pot in front of me, with Mrs Imani chatting away, like usual, things felt okay again. In fact, it was easy to forget that anything had changed at all. The other kids in my class did seem to get used to it pretty quickly, and they were calling me Alison in no time.

It wasn't until recess that the uneasiness crept back in. It was all the stares and the hushed whispers. Kids who had heard what had happened telling those who hadn't. I hurried over to the bench where I always meet up with Savannah and the others. I was the first there, so I sat down and tried to ignore all the sideways glances.

Where were they? The minutes ticked by and I was still sitting on my own. All the other children were playing with their friends, laughing and smiling in their own bodies. It just wasn't fair.

My eyes were drawn to some commotion over on the field. A group of kids had gathered underneath a tree. When I noticed a flash of red hair, I decided to go and check it out.

Nearing the crowd, I looked up, following everyone's amused gazes. One of the school's security drones was stuck in the tree and a small boy had climbed halfway up the trunk, trying to knock it down. He couldn't seem to get close enough.

I walked up to Savannah, Mikaela and Grace.

"What's happening?" I asked.

"He's never going to get it," Grace said. "He's not tall enough."

Savannah smiled at me, her eyebrows raised. "You should go up, Ali. You'll be able to reach it in that body."

I looked up. The drone's blades were not moving, but it was pretty high up. If you fell from there you'd really hurt yourself.

"That's a great idea," Mikaela said. "It doesn't matter if you injure that body. They'll get you a new one."

"But it would hurt!" I said, not liking where this was going or the way they were looking at me. "And anyway, shouldn't we just tell a teacher? A maintenance droid could get it down in no time."

"Where's the fun in that?" Savannah said, scowling slightly. Then she called up to the kid in the tree. "Hey, come down! Ali will have a go."

Everyone nodded and smiled, as though it was the best idea ever. I just stood there, Savannah, Mikaela and Grace all staring at me, eyebrows raised. What was I supposed to do? Climbing trees wasn't really my thing. In fact, I hadn't done it since I was little and me and Olivia used to climb the big tree in her garden. That was a very long time ago.

The boy was down now, so I made my way to the base of the trunk. Even more kids had gathered round to see how high the clone could get. The lump in my throat told me that this wasn't a good idea. But it was too late. Everyone was staring at me, waiting for me to start climbing.

I grabbed one of the lower branches and pulled myself up, trying to ignore my fear by focusing on my breath as it wheezed in and out of my nostrils. One branch at a time. Breathe in. Breathe out.

The drone got closer, but the ground was getting further and further below. I glanced beyond the drone, hoping to catch a glimpse of an LPD hovering close by, but could only see blue sky scattered with clouds. If I fell from here, I might well need Life Preservation. But what would happen if I damaged this clone? Would they even give me a new one?

I'd made it much higher than the boy had, but still the drone was out of reach. With my left hand gripping the thickest branch I could find, I leaned out, stretching towards the drone as far as I could. It was about a metre away, so I moved up to a slightly flimsier part of the branch. My breaths were screeching through my nostrils so loudly that I was sure the spectators could hear them.

Fifty centimetres now. Still too far. But I could reach a twig from the drone's branch, so I looped my index finger around it and gave it a little shake. The drone quivered. I shook again, harder this time. The drone shifted a few inches. There were cheers from the spectators below, but I was doing everything I could to block them out. I was close. Just one more shake would do it.

I pulled myself upright to adjust my grip on the branch.

"Come on, Ali! You can do it."

"Don't worry about falling. It's only a clone body."

I stretched forwards again and was just about to grab the same twig when I heard a teacher's voice. Not just any teacher, either. It was Mrs Imani. "Who's up... Alison Greene! Get down from there this instant. One accident in a week is more than enough, young lady."

Her voice made me jump and my foot slipped. The next thing I knew I was dangling amongst the leaves, gripping a branch with my left hand while my right flailed around for something to grab onto.

The bark dug into my fingers as they slowly slipped apart. Just before I fell, my right hand caught hold of a branch. I swung my legs onto the closest part of the trunk and gripped it like a koala bear, my heart pounding so loudly in my ears that it blocked out all the excited chatter below.

By the time I had lowered myself back down to the ground, most of the crowd had dispersed. Savannah and the others were nowhere to be seen. Not that I'd have been able to stay and chat. Before I was led away, I did notice the security camera drone, though. It was lying on the grass at the base of the tree, completely intact. I'd actually done it. I got it down.

Mrs Imani kept a firm grip on my upper arm as she marched me over to the classroom. She closed the door behind us, then gestured for me to sit.

I sat.

She just stood there next to me. Staring down at my clone body without saying anything for at least thirty seconds. My heart had stopped its super-thumping, but my breath was still wheezing in and out of my nostrils.

"I expect better behaviour than that from you, young lady. You could have really hurt yourself." She took a few deep breaths in through *her* nose, as though calming herself down. "It will be difficult enough in a clone's body for a month or two. You don't want to add a couple of broken legs into the equation."

I hadn't thought about that. Sure, if it had been life or death the LPDs would have saved me. But broken limbs still have to mend the old-fashioned way. In good time.

Mrs Imani stared deep into my eyes, her hand placed gently on my shoulder. "Now, if any of your *friends* can't handle you looking like that, they might not be worthy of the title."

At home that evening, while we were having dinner, Mum asked her usual question.

"So, how was school today?"

"Fine," I said, giving my standard response.

"It didn't look fine," Luke said. "She nearly fell out of a tree while trying to rescue a drone. Half the school was watching."

My brother's great like that. He sat there with a smug expression on his face, while Mum and Dad stared at me, eyebrows raised.

"It wasn't a big deal," I said, my eyes drilling so hard into Luke I was surprised it didn't hurt him. "Someone needed to get a security drone out of the tree, so I climbed up and got it. No sweat."

"You volunteered to be the one to climb the tree?" Dad asked, his clone-head tilted to the side.

"Yeah."

Mum and Dad exchanged glances. A silence hung in the air for a few moments. I focused on stabbing peas with my fork.

"Oh..." Mum said, clearly wanting to change the subject. "I got a call from the rehabilitation clinic today. They want us to visit your body tomorrow, so I thought we'd go after school."

"Why do I need to visit my own body?"

"It helps to prepare you for any physical changes, you know, from the accident."

"What kind of physical changes?"

"Scars mostly. Or swelling. Perhaps reduced movement in certain areas."

It was funny. Until that moment, I hadn't even wondered how my own body was. I'd been so preoccupied with being stuck in this stupid clone, I hadn't given it any thought.

"Is my body okay?"

"It was pretty banged up," Dad said. "Even worse than mine. Yours took the full force of the impact."

I suddenly had a squirmy, wriggling feeling in my tummy, as though I wasn't going to like what I saw. What if my face was all disfigured? Or one of my limbs was missing? That would be even worse than being in a clone.

"We thought you might like to bring a friend along," Mum added. "You know, to give you some support."

Maybe I could ask Savannah? Surely she'd be happy to come along.

I didn't sleep very well that night. All the things that might be wrong with my body kept playing on my mind. I imagined it looked like Frankenstein's monster lying in a hospital bed.

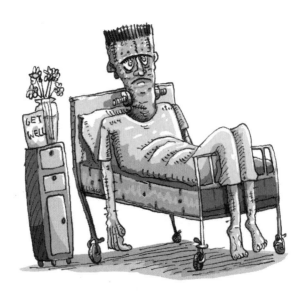

What would Savannah say to that? Would she still want to be my friend if I had scars and deformities? If I was no longer pretty?

The next day at school was a bit of a blur. I kept trying to find the right time to ask Savannah to come to the clinic with me, but she was always with one of the others and it never felt quite right. It was almost like she was avoiding me. As though she couldn't bear to spend time with me in my clone body.

When home time came around I figured I'd just have to ask her, regardless of who she was with. I walked around the playground with my bag slung over my shoulder, looking for the familiar red hair.

I eventually found her in the lower part of the school grounds, at the top of the flight of steps that leads down to the car park. She was with Mikaela and Grace, and I could instantly tell they were up to something.

"Oh, Ali-clone's here," Savannah said, a big smile breaking out on her face. "She'll have a go!"

"Have a go at what?" I didn't like the sound of this.

"We're going to see who can slide all the way down the handrail. Right to the bottom."

I glanced down the concrete steps. It was a very long way down. And we were specifically forbidden from sliding on the railing, ever since Henry Harman broke his arm and gave himself concussion.

"I'm not doing that!" I said, the words popping out before I could stop them. "It's dangerous!"

"What does that matter?" Savannah asked, her eyes narrowing. "You're only in a clone's body, anyway. And I can see an LPD hovering just up there, so it's not like we'd die or anything."

I squinted up at the sky. Sure enough, there was a small black dot up high, waiting for someone to have a life-threatening injury.

"We're going to do it," Savannah said, turning to the other two girls. "Aren't we, Grace?"

Grace swallowed and nodded.

"It's not a good idea," I said. "You could really hurt yourself."

"Nah, it'll be fine," Grace said, stepping up to the railing, her eyes focused on the ground.

There were other kids walking past, heading down to the car park. But no one took any notice when Grace popped her bum up on the handrail and lifted her legs. She held her arms out for balance and whizzed down the slope. About a quarter of the way down she wobbled and came off, landing on her feet and jumping down several steps.

She beamed up at us with a huge grin, obviously very proud of herself for not dying.

I couldn't watch any more.

"I'm going home," I said, turning around and walking back up towards the school buildings. It looked like I'd have to go to the rehab clinic on my own.

I could hear the girls laughing and calling after me, but I just ignored them. I wasn't going to break the rules just because my friends told me to. It was like Mrs Imani had said. Maybe they weren't worthy.

The school playground was thinning out now as people made their way home. Luke's friends were playing football on the field, like usual. Luke was probably there somewhere. He was always late getting home.

I was just about to head for the top gate when I saw Olivia walking out of the library. You couldn't miss her big heavy shoes. And her bag looked heavy too. It was probably loaded with books. She made her way towards the gate without seeing me.

I jogged after her.

"Hey Olivia, wait!" When she looked up and saw me her face broke into a smile, even though she'd just have seen a pale-faced clone with a shaved head. "Can I walk home with you?"

She nodded, her smile going even wider. "Of course you can, Alison. Anytime."

As we walked, just chatting about stuff like the old days, things felt normal. Then I had a thought.

"Hey, umm, I was wondering..." I said, struggling to find the words. "I've got to go to the rehab clinic tonight. To see my body for the first time after the crash. Did you, umm, want to come with me?"

"Yeah, I'll definitely come," she said, nodding. Then her forehead wrinkled in concern. "How are you feeling about it?"

"I don't know. Okay, I guess. Whatever state it's in, it's got to be better than this stupid body." My throat tightened as I said this, because it wasn't really true, was it? Things could be much worse. Permanently.

But suddenly, I knew something for certain. Olivia wouldn't mind if I had scars or missing pieces. She'd be friends with me, even if I was stuck in this clone body for ever. I just wished I could say the same for Savannah.

As I thought of Savannah, a high-pitched buzz cut through the air. Olivia and I both looked up as a Life Preservation Drone shot down from the sky and headed straight for the school grounds. The lower part of the school. By the steps.

There was a sinking feeling in my stomach. I had a pretty good idea what might have happened. Perhaps I wouldn't be the only clone in school, after all.

Not that it would change anything. From now on, I'm going to choose friends that are worthy of the title. Like Olivia.

IN AGREEMENT

When I was little, my mum was the most magical storyteller. The way she pulled you inside the story, the words she crafted and the voices she used would grab you from the very beginning.

But she never began with 'Once upon a time' or 'One day'. Her stories always started with 'This story begins...'

From those words on, she could make even the most farfetched tale seem like it really happened. And she seemed to know – or make up – hundreds of stories about witches and magic and everything you can think of.

But there was one story that I loved more than any other. I would beg her to tell it to me every night. "Please, Mum," I'd say. "The one about the cockroaches." Mum would smile her knowing smile and begin the story. This story. I can't promise I'll tell it as well as my mum, even though I've certainly heard it enough times.

So here we go.

This story begins when Roland Spragg arrived home from work, jingling his keys (Mum would always jingle her own keys for effect at this point). A gust of wet wind followed him through the doorway, toppling birthday cards off the mantelpiece and riffling its way through his daughter Miranda's homework book. Mr Spragg gripped the heavy door in both hands and pushed with all the force he could muster. For a moment it seemed the wind would be victorious, but with a grunt from Mr Spragg, the door clicked closed and rain scurried across the glass panel like the patter of tiny feet.

"I did it!" Mr Spragg announced. (And here Mum would use a deep booming voice.) "I gloopin' well did it!"

He wiped a wet strand of hair from his forehead and shuffled his feet on the doormat.

"Well done, Dad," Miranda said, releasing her grip on her homework book. "For a moment, I thought the wind would win, but you really showed it who's boss!"

Roland Spragg scrunched up his face. "What in the drivellation... no! Not that. I evicted them. I finally got rid of that disgustable family of leeches."

Mr Spragg's wife, Patricia, rushed over with a fresh towel. "Well done, dear," she said, dabbing at the bald patch atop Mr Spragg's head. "I knew you could do it."

"Well, it certastically wasn't easy," he said, slipping the wet trench coat from his shoulders and holding it out to his wife. "But that's the last of those money-sucking parasotes in my properties. From now on we'll be getting three hundred and fifty dollars per room, not per stinkling house."

"How *did* you do it, Dad?"

"I just told 'em I was sub-divisling their property and handered them their new agreement." He dabbed the hair above his ears with the towel. "If they was intendering to stay, they'd need to pay four times their usual rent at noon tomorrow. And we all know they can't plauserly have one thousand four hundred dollars stashed away. Even if today *is* a very rainy day."

He threw his head back and let out a deep, bellowing laugh. (And I wish you could hear Mum's bellowing laugh. It was awesome!)

"Is this the lady with the cute little boy, Dad?"

"My backside is cuter than that snivellatious little roach." Mr Spragg slapped his thigh and laughed at his own joke once again. "Little darlin', she called 'im. 'What will I do with my little darlin'?' she says. Like I'm supposed to know. Then she starts cursing me this and spelling me that. 'I already am cursed,' I says, 'having you wretching roaches in my property.'"

Miranda's mouth dropped open. "But where are they supposed to go, Dad?"

"How the henkling should I know?" Mr Spragg said, scowling at his impertinent daughter. "Thankingfully, that is no longer my problem."

Patricia Spragg ushered her husband towards the dining table. "Come sit down, my heroic, handsome husband," she said, removing the lid of a serving dish. A cloud of steam escaped from a golden roast chicken. "I've cooked your favourite."

Alfie sat in his highchair at the head of the table, his spoon and fork clutched in his chubby fists.

"I evictivated that lady today, Little Man," Mr Spragg said, plopping himself down directly opposite his son.

"Gagga!" Alfie said, banging his spoon on the table.

Mr Spragg smiled fondly. *It will all be yours one day, son*, he thought. *All this property and wealth. And I suppose Miranda should get some, too. Although she'd probably give it all to some worthingless charity.*

"Well, I think you should let them stay," Miranda said, looking at her brother fondly. "It's not like we need the money, Dad. And they definitely need a roof over their heads."

Mr Spragg slowly turned towards his daughter, his face going as red as a stop sign.

"WE DON'T NEED THE MONEY?" Mr Spragg yelled, his voice a bit squeakier than usual. "How the heckling do you think we pay for all this food? With kind words?"

He looks quite small today, Miranda thought. *Like he's shrunk under the weight of his actions.* Then she looked at Alfie and her eyes widened. He had definitely shrunk. His head didn't even reach the tray of his highchair. *How can that possibly be?*

Miranda gripped the plate in front of her. It felt massive all of a sudden, like it had tripled in size.

There was a knock at the door. (Here Mum would knock on the closest surface, making you jump.)

Everyone turned in that direction, but Miranda couldn't see the entranceway. Her view was obscured by the serving dish. She glanced to the left and stared wide-eyed at her dad.

He was now standing on the edge of the table, no bigger than a garden gnome. His face still glowed red, but the rest of his body had turned a deep brown colour.

His arms narrowed before her eyes and another set of limbs protruded from his middle. He continued to get smaller, his body curling over and flattening out until he lost all resemblance to his normal self. Instead, perched on the edge of his plate, was a big fat cockroach.

Miranda glanced around, looking for the rest of her family, but they were gone too. Disappeared.

Instead, there was another cockroach clinging to the tray on Alfie's highchair. And a third scurrying around in circles where Mrs Spragg had been standing only seconds ago.

It took Miranda a moment to realise that she too had turned into a cockroach. As she looked around, a pair of spindly antennae quivered and waved in her line of sight. The dishes on the table towered above her and the ceiling was way up in the sky.

The front door opened, inviting in a gust of wind. The pages of Miranda's homework book fluttered and flapped with no hand to hold it closed.

"Hello?" a soft voice called, and a head with long dark hair peered around the doorway. "In you come, Duke. Our new home is ready."

Water puddled on the floorboards as the lady and her five-year-old son stepped into the house.

(This was something Mum often did in her stories. She'd feature herself as a beautiful and magical lady, and me as a small child.)

Silvia Boswell placed two enormous suitcases on the floor and turned around. Pressing both hands firmly on the door, she forced it closed and the wind died down with a click of the latch.

"Wow, Mummy ... this is amazing," Duke said, wiping water from his forehead with the back of his hand.

"Take your shoes and raincoat off, please," Silvia said. "We don't want to mess up our new home before we've even settled in."

Miranda watched all this from the rim of her plate. Who were these people and what were they doing in their house? And, more importantly, how on earth had her entire family turned into cockroaches? It just didn't make sense.

Mr Spragg – or the cockroach formerly known as Mr Spragg – stood motionless on his six legs. He knew very well who these people were. He had seen Ms Boswell only hours before, when he'd kicked her and the child out of his rental property. And that evil lady's cursings and mutterings had indeed contained the word 'cockroach'. But how dare she do this to his family? Who the heckling did she think she was?

"How wonderful. Dinner is on the table already," Silvia said, as she strolled across the room. "Come sit up, my little darlin'. You must be famished."

"Ooh, gross! There are bugs here, too," said Duke, as he spotted Mr Spragg standing in the middle of his plate. The cockroach stared at the intruders with every ounce of hatred in his little body. Until he saw Duke approach him, rolling up Miranda's homework book. As his enormous arm rose into the air, its weapon the size of a train carriage, Mr Spragg's anger turned into fear. He darted forwards on his six legs and leapt off the edge of the plate, just as

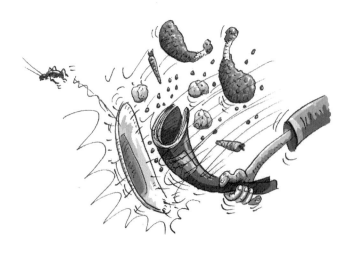

the rolled-up book came crashing down with an almighty thump. The plate wobbled from side to side, sending reverberations through the table.

Miranda quietly slipped under the rim of her plate as her father scurried to the safety of the serving dishes. At the other end of the table, Alfie stood on six wobbly legs. Duke lifted up the edge of the plate and dropped it down on top of the small bug.

NO! thought Miranda. *Poor little Alfie.* The plate rose up into the air, revealing the tiny cockroach lying motionless on his back. Duke reached out his chunky finger and flicked him off the table. Alfie thudded into the back of his highchair, then came to rest on its seat, his six legs splayed out in different directions.

Miranda turned away, shocked. *He can't be dead. Surely. Please let him be okay!*

The sight of the golden roast chicken halted the bug hunt. The boy clambered onto a chair as Silvia Boswell dolloped large helpings of steaming meat and vegetables onto each of their plates.

"It's like Christmas!" said Duke, rubbing his hands together.

Silvia smiled. Yes, it was very much like Christmas. And Scrooge had given them the best gift of all.

Miranda spent the entire meal cowering under the rim of Duke's plate. Luckily for her, he was a messy eater, so she was able to nibble at some of the crumbs and spillages. But time ambled past. All she could think about was what had happened and why. She figured this must be the lady that Dad had kicked out of his rental property. And hadn't he mentioned a curse? But the big question was whether or not the curse could be undone. And what could Miranda do about it? After all, she certainly

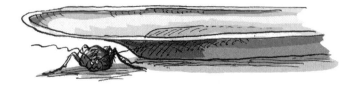

didn't want to spend the rest of her life as a cockroach, hiding in the dark and dirty corners of her own home.

"Are we going to live here forever, Mum?" Duke asked, as a second helping was dolloped onto his plate. "Can we?"

"We'll have to see, dear," Silvia said, carving off another slice of chicken. "I'd much rather be in our old place. That is our home, after all."

"But I thought that man said we can't live there any more," Duke replied through a mouthful of potato.

Silvia smiled. Her little darlin' was so wonderful. So deserving of the very best. "I'm hoping he has a change of heart," she said, pulling a piece of paper from her pocket. She unfolded it and stared at the ridiculous sum at the bottom of the new rental agreement. "I'd move back in right away, if he were to return the rent to what it used to be."

She placed the paper at the end of the table, laid a pen on top of it, then picked up her knife and fork. After cutting off a piece of chicken, she chewed thoughtfully for a moment.

Miranda watched all of this from her position under the rim of the plate. She could also see her father, a dark shape cowering in the shadow of the bowl of vegetables. Could he see the piece of paper from there? Had he listened to that conversation? Miranda wasn't one hundred per cent sure, but she thought there might be a way to fix this. If she could get Dad to change the lady's rent back, then maybe she would make them human again.

At that moment the plate above her was lifted into the air and Miranda was suddenly exposed on the table top. She quickly scurried to the centre where her dad was hiding underneath the veggie dish. He looked up when he saw her squeeze into the gap. His antennae twitched and quivered, and amazingly, she could understand what he meant. "Oh, Miranda," he waved and swirled. "Thank Godness you're okay!"

"I'm fine, Dad," Miranda said, her antennae etching the understanding out of thin air. "But we have to do something! We must get these people out of our house!"

Mr Spragg's antennae were still, but his front right leg tapped nervously.

"This can't be happening," he said, swaying his head from side to side. "That lady. That harrible witch. She did this to us. How dare she..."

Mr Spragg stopped mid-sentence, his body flopping forward. "It's all my fault. I never should have increasled their rent. If only I hadn't been so greedy. But it's too late now. We are worthingless cockroaches."

Miranda glanced from the hunched and sorry shape of her father over to the piece of paper at the other end of the table. In reality it wasn't far away, but it felt like the opposite end of a netball court. A netball court surrounded by giants wielding enormous weapons.

"There might be a way to fix this," Miranda said, as a shadow loomed over them. The vegetable dish – their only shelter – was lifted into the air.

"Yuck, here's two more of 'em," Duke said, peering over the top of the peas and carrots. "Where's that swatter?"

Duke swiped the homework book up from the counter and rolled it into a lethal weapon.

"Follow me, Dad!" Miranda said, then she turned and darted across the table, her tiny body swelling with fear. Her eyes seemed to have hundreds of little segments, so she could take the whole room in at once. She could see the piece of paper up ahead, her father scurrying behind and Duke raising the homework book high above his head.

Mum always said that homework wouldn't kill me, thought Miranda, as weeks of hard work descended upon her like a falling building. *Perhaps she was wrong.*

She could sense movements in the air and her body automatically put out a blast of speed. There was a deafening thump and the table shook like an earthquake. *Dad!* thought Miranda. *Please, no!*

The piece of paper loomed up before her, so Miranda slipped under its edge and spun around. She was just in time to see the homework book come swooping down again. Her father was scuttling towards her as fast as he could, but it wasn't fast enough. He tried darting to the side, but the homework book was too big and crashed down on the table, completely obscuring him.

Duke lifted his weapon up and examined its underside, expecting to see the remains of a cockroach. Mr Spragg lay in the middle of the table, unmoving.

Miranda watched all this from beneath her flimsy shelter. Her father didn't move. Not even the faintest twitch of antenna or leg.

No! He didn't make it.

Duke rolled the book tighter, getting it ready to finish him off. Miranda couldn't watch.

"Come on, Duke," Silvia Boswell called from the kitchen, "you can dry the dishes."

"But, Mum, I'm..."

"No buts. Get here right now, young man."

Casting a final glance at the motionless cockroach, Duke spun on his heel and stomped towards the kitchen, flinging the homework book onto the counter along the way.

Miranda rushed over to her father, who still lay motionless on his back.

"Dad?" she said, poking him with her front right leg. "Get up. We need to fix this."

Mr Spragg's antennae quivered in the cockroach equivalent of a groan.

"Dad?" Miranda said again. "Please don't be dead."

She placed both her front legs underneath her father's thorax and pushed, flipping him onto his feet. His antennae continued to tremble and his two rear legs twitched.

"Mirannnhhha?" Mr Spragg slurred, as Miranda pushed him along the table towards the rental agreement. "Wha happa?"

"You got hit. By spelling and multiplication practice. But we're safe for a few moments while they do the dishes."

"Am I still a disgustling cockroach?"

"Yes, but try to walk. I think I know a way to fix it."

Clattering and clinking came from the kitchen as Mr Spragg and his daughter scurried across the tabletop. When they reached the large piece of paper, Miranda led the way onto, rather than under, the sheet. Huge letters stretched across the page, almost impossible to read from Miranda's position.

She focused hard and could make out the words *legally binding contract*. She crawled down the page, past *fixed-term tenancy,* until she found *rent per week* in huge letters. Next to that it said *1,400 dollars.*

"Here it is, Dad," Miranda said. "We just need to change the amount back to what it was."

Mr Spragg wobbled over, his six legs getting tangled up with each other.

"Are you sure...?"

"Yes, I am sure!" Miranda said, jabbing at the air with her front leg. "Unless you want us to spend the rest of our lives as cockroaches. Getting swatted in our own home."

"But how am I changeling it?"

Miranda glanced at the pen lying across the page like a fallen tree trunk. Its nib contained a huge sphere the size of a beach ball covered in a gloppy blue substance. *Ink!*

She scuttled over and scooped some ink off with one of the pointy bits on her foot. She carefully walked on five legs back to her father, who was still standing next to the *1,400 dollars*. Miranda reached out with her inky foot and put a line through the *dollar sign*, *one* and *four*. By then the ink had run out, so she went back and grabbed another footful.

"Help me, would you?" Miranda said to her father, who was swaying slightly where he stood, as though six legs weren't enough to keep him steady.

His head segment shuddered, then Mr Spragg staggered over to the pen and grabbed himself a scoop of ink. By the time he got back, Miranda had already written the dollar sign.

"How much should it be?" Miranda asked as she scurried off to get more ink.

"I ... I ... I can't recollection," said Mr Spragg, still dazed from his near-fatal blow. "Either 250 dollars or 350 dollars."

"Let's go with 250," said Miranda, starting with the curve at the top and only getting halfway through the first long straight before running out of ink. "The happier that lady is, the more likely she'll put things back to normal."

Mr Spragg finished off the *2*, while Miranda went back to the pen for more ink. The gurgle and splutter of a sink draining came from the kitchen, as Miranda did the top half of the *5*, then Mr Spragg finished it off.

The stomp of enormous feet approaching sent vibrations through the table. Silvia Boswell strode across the room, a pink dishcloth scrunched in her hand. She leaned over the table, carefully sweeping crumbs and discarded chunks of vegetables into her other hand. Her eyes flashed over the cockroaches on the sheet of paper as she wiped around them, the edges of her mouth curling into a smile. She turned and strolled back to the kitchen, not wanting to interrupt her busy hosts.

Miranda and Mr Spragg finished the *0* and stepped back to admire their handiwork. The dollar sign and the two were a little wobbly,

but it was completely legible and you'd never know it wasn't penned by human hand.

"Holdle a moment..." Mr Spragg said, tilting his head to the side. "It needs one more thing."

He loaded up with more ink, then wrote his initials above the new sum.

As his foot came around the final swerve of the *S*, a call came from the kitchen. "Okay Duke, grab your things. We're off in one minute."

"But, Muuuum, can't we stay?" Duke whined. "This place is awesome."

"It's not our house, so its owners could be back at any moment," she said, sliding her arm into the sleeve of her coat as she walked over towards the table once again.

Miranda and Mr Spragg stepped off the sheet of paper, their eyes fixed on the enormous woman towering over them. She swept the rental agreement from the table, her eyes scanning the text. She nodded approvingly, then turned and strode towards the door, without so much as a glance at the two cockroaches.

Wind swept through the house once again, rustling the leaves of the pot plants and rifling through the pages of the homework book that had nearly killed Mr Spragg. The door clicked shut, leaving behind a silence that was warm and welcome.

Mr Spragg's mind felt even more fuddled, all of a sudden. The table seemed much smaller. And his antennae appeared to be retracting back into his body.

As she looked down at her spindly cockroach legs, Miranda watched human fingers pop out of the ends, one at a time, until she was looking at two tiny hands that got bigger and bigger before her eyes. The room around them looked like it was shrinking, the ceiling getting lower.

A moment later, Mr Spragg and Miranda were both human again, sitting side by side on top of the table. Mr Spragg clutched his head in both hands and groaned. He'd never had a headache quite that bad before.

Miranda glanced around the room. Her mum was lying in the fetal position beside the wall and Alfie sat in his highchair, slumping forward against the tray. For a moment Miranda thought he might not have made it, but he lifted his head and scanned the room, a jubilant smile spreading across his face.

For a while, no one spoke. No one stood up. They all just stared around the room, attempting to process what had happened.

"I just had the most awful dream," Mrs Spragg said, breaking the silence. "It was ... we were..." Her fingers moved over the contours of her face, checking that everything was back as it should be.

Miranda looked at her dad.

His shoulders were hunched forward and the angry-redness of his face had faded. He closed his eyes and took a deep breath through his nose.

Exhaling slowly, he opened his eyes and gave Miranda a half-smile. He then reached out and took her hand, holding it gently for the first time that she could remember.

"I think we should look at how much you're charging your other tenants," she said softly.

Her dad nodded vigorously.

"For once," he said, "I'm in agreement."

At this point, Mum would say, "The end," as she folded her arms and smiled. She did this throughout my childhood and even when she told me her stories as an adult. Then, when I had children of my own, she'd tell them the same stories. All the way up to The End, when she died last week.

I'd never even considered the idea that there might be any truth behind her stories. Surely they were just magical tales that she'd made up.

But then a tall, elegant lady walked up to me at Mum's funeral. She seemed somehow familiar, but I couldn't work out where I'd seen her before.

She smiled and said, "Hi, Duke, you look just like you did when you were a boy."

I smiled back, staring at her blankly, my hand instinctively going to the bald patch on top of my head.

"I just wanted to pay my respects to your mother," she said, bowing her head. "She did more for our company than she'll ever know."

Then she handed me a business card, smiled again and slipped back into the crowd.

I stared at the card in my hand.

Suddenly, I'm not so sure where real life ends and Mum's stories begin.

"Aren't you nervous?" I ask, peering around my computer screen.

Josh glances up from his comic book. He looks more like he's waiting to get a haircut than about to sit the most important test of his life.

"Nah," he says, "this is going to be *une morceau de gateau!*"

My jaw drops open.

"But…" I stammer, "they could test us on anything we've learnt over the last five years!"

"Yeah?" says Josh. "I know all that!"

How can anyone be so relaxed before an exam that determines what job you're going to have for the rest of your life? "But there's even an astrophysics section!" I say.

"Yep."

"And Mr Parsons says there'll be a section on palaeontology this year!"

Josh's eyes widen.

"Palaeontology?" he asks. "Really? That wasn't in the study list."

"Yeah, I know." I'm glad there's at least one part of the Sixth Grade Life Test that makes him nervous. "Mr Parsons said they added it recently, just to catch people out."

Josh chews his lip.

"Cedric, can I use your computer?" he asks.

Without waiting for my reply he slides along the bench, leans over and types 'masterminds.com' into Google.

He pulls up a website I've never seen before. It has thumbnail pictures of hundreds of people, each with a brief description of their achievements below the image.

Josh types 'palaeontology' into the search bar and it refines the search to eight images.

"Which of these looks best?" he asks.

I scan the page, glancing over the faces and picking out keywords in the bios. All the people sound pretty knowledgeable, but Dr Ralph Holmes has both the longest description and the longest beard.

"It says this guy has got two doctorate degrees ... one in palaeontology and one in micro-palaeontology!"

"Perfect," Josh says, and he clicks on the image.

He leans over and carefully pulls a strange device out of his backpack. It's like a set of headphones but it has all these electrodes hanging off it. Josh puts the headphones on, then one by one fastens the electrodes to his forehead and temples. Once he's ready, he plugs into the USB port on my computer.

On the screen, directly under the image of a brain, there's a button that says *Upload Mind*.

Josh clicks it, then closes his eyes. His face twitches as a progress bar slowly fills up.

There's a ping and my screen says, *Upload Complete*, but Josh still doesn't open his eyes.

I put my hand on his shoulder and give him a little shake.

"Josh? Are you all right?"

My breathing speeds up. A glance at my watch tells me it's 08:49, so the test starts in ten minutes. Josh can't afford to miss it. None of us can. Not if we want bright futures.

I give him another shake. Harder this time.

He opens his eyes suddenly, as if he just woke up from a deep sleep.

"Josh?" I ask again. "Are you okay?"

"I'm not Josh," he says in a monotone. "I'm Albert, Gottfried, Isaac, Leonardo, John, Galileo, Rene, Desiderius ... and Ralph."

"But..." I say, my heart pounding in my chest, "we've got the test in ten minutes."

"*Solo dieci minuti!*" Josh says with more emotion in his voice. "*Das sind sechshundert sekunden.* Which is approximately six hundred thousand milliseconds... More than enough time to sing a song!" He stands up and starts singing in a foreign language.

Other kids are glancing at him as they make their way into the hall, but they're too worried about their own futures to pay him much attention. What am I going to do? I can't leave Josh like this.

I quickly open Google and type 'Uploaded Mastermind. Now talking rubbish.'

Thousands of hits come up on the screen. Way too many to read. I catch glimpses of things like *Disconnect electrodes* and *seek immediate medical assistance.*

What has Josh done to himself?

I keep scanning through the search results. I can't take him to a doctor now. He'll miss the test. I need to fix him, but I only have eight minutes to do it.

Then my eyes land on a search item that says *Mastermind overload Quickhack.*

That's exactly what I need.

I click on it and see the following intro:

Has someone you know overloaded themselves with Mastermind knowledge? Are they now talking gibberish and answering to

*multiple names? At quickhack.com we can help
you get them back to normal. Simply enter
your Paypal details below and select the most
appropriate Quickhack operator from our
database.*

Okay, okay. That sounds perfect. There are
six minutes until the start of the test and Josh
and I are the only people left in the waiting
area. I have to do this. I fumble with my phone
to find Dad's Paypal details and quickly enter
them.

Payment confirmed. Please select operator.

The screen pops up with a whole load of
thumbnails, just like on masterminds.com. But
these guys don't look quite as clever as the last
lot. Half the people in the photos are wearing
dark sunglasses or have tattoos creeping up
their neck.

One is called Nice Guy Eddie. He doesn't look
so bad. It says he has 360 degrees from the
University of Life and he loves to help the
hapless. He's wearing a suit and tie, without

sunglasses. And there are no visible tattoos in the photo.

I click on his image and the screen flashes up the words *'Attach electrodes'*. There's a diagram showing where they need to go.

"Pour mon-âme, quel destin!" Josh wails. He is now on his hands and knees examining a piece of chewing gum that's stuck to the floor, like he's just discovered an alien substance. He scratches at it with his nail then dabs a bit on the end of his tongue.

- **NICE GUY EDDIE** -
STEER CLEAR OF ALL
THESE OTHER SCUMBAGS

I pluck the electrodes from his head one at a time, but Josh doesn't even notice. He just carries on singing.

"J'ai sa flamme, et j'ai main!"

I make sure there is no one else around, then stick the electrodes onto my own forehead. Once they are on I have a strange feeling in my chest, like I'm doing something I shouldn't. But how else am I supposed to fix Josh? And the test is going to begin in a few moments.

Before I change my mind I quickly tap the download button. I suddenly have the sensation that my head is filling with cold liquid. It feels incredible. I close my eyes, just to hold onto the feeling for as long as possible. The last thing I see on the screen is a skull and crossbones image above the words *Your mind is being hacked by Nice Guy Eddie.*

I think I've just made a very big mistake.

As soon as my mind takes over the new body I open my eyes a fraction and have a peek around. I'm in a lobby area with high ceilings and wooden floors. Judging by the uncomfortable benches and 'Quiet Please'

signs it must be a school. And I'm in a young boy's body, which makes sense. It is Life Test day, after all.

There's another boy on his hands and knees in front of me. He's scraped up a piece of pre-chewed gum and is rolling it around in his fingers. He's probably going to pop it in his mouth, the idiot. It doesn't take a genius to work out that he's been messing with masterminds.com. It looks like he's two or three minds over capacity.

I quickly pull the electrodes off my host's head and stuff them into the other boy's pocket. He's so jelly-brained he doesn't even notice.

An expensive digital watch with too many buttons tells me that it's 08:58. Perfect. The Life Test is about to start, so everyone will be too preoccupied to worry about me.

I open up this kid's Paypal account and check the

balance. A measly seventy-nine dollars, but it's better than nothing. It takes me less than thirty seconds to transfer it into an offshore bank account. This is all too easy.

"Why are you two still out here?" A teacher with pink ribbons in her bushy hair stands in the double doorway. She looks like a poodle as she stares at us with her hands on her hips, like we're breaking the law or something. "The test starts in one minute!"

"So? What do I care?" I say, closing the laptop and shoving it into this kid's bag. "You don't need a bunch of useless facts to survive on the street. You just need your wits and your cunning!"

Jelly Brain looks pretty low on wits and cunning at the moment. I'd better get out of here before he gives us away.

"Facts are the foundations of intelligence!" Jelly Brain says before he gets up and starts walking towards the test hall. That is really not a good idea. Word on the street is that all schools have been fitted with tamper sensors.

Alarms will tamper with everyone's eardrums if Jelly Brain enters that hall.

"That's very true, Joshua," Mrs Poodle says, grabbing him by the wrist and leading him towards the double doors. I can't decide whether to stop them or leg it.

I'll stop them. It's better for me if the tamper alarms don't go off.

"Let him go!" I call out. "You're using physical force on a student. I'm going to call the police!" I get the boy's phone out of my pocket and hold my finger above the screen, as if I were about to dial the emergency number. As if!

"What on earth has gotten into you, Cedric? You know the importance of this test. Get in here immediately or I will call your mum."

Cedric? Oh dear, oh dear. What were his parents thinking? That's even worse than my own real name. I thought I had it tough as a kid, but with a name like Cedric he might as well have a bull's-eye tattooed on his forehead.

I'm almost tempted to wait around to meet the parents. If they're stupid enough to name their kid Cedric it might be easy to extract a few bucks from them.

But I'm pretty sure she's bluffing. The bigger concern is the fact that Mrs Poodle and Jelly Brain are now extremely close to the test-hall doors.

I consider grabbing hold of Jelly Brain's other arm and having a quick tug of war to stop him going through those doors. But there must be over two hundred kids on the other side, all in silence. It's not worth causing that much of a scene. And anyway, in this scrawny boy's body, I'd probably be dragged through the doors and everyone would know that his brain has been tampered with too. I'm better off heading back to Cedric's house while every other kid in the country is doing their exam. Perhaps there's some jewellery that I could stash in a public locker. Or maybe some cash or bank cards. That way I'll be able to retrieve them once I'm back in my own body.

I turn away from the test hall and walk calmly towards the exit. Before I'm even halfway there I hear the tamper alarms going off. I pick up speed, head down, eyes on the floor. Daylight is spilling through the door, illuminating my route to freedom. But then someone steps in front of the doorway, blocking out half the light. The flash of a security badge is enough for me to spin around and try a different escape route.

Up ahead, Jelly Brain has his hands up against the wall and another security guard is waving a mind probe around his head. He's been well and truly busted. I pick up speed but the guard is right behind me and there doesn't seem to be another exit. I'm going to have to bluff my way out of this one.

I slam on the brakes and brace myself. The security guard crashes into me and I dive forward, rolling across the floor and grimacing as if it really hurt. I clutch my head with both hands.

"Ow, my head!"

The guard is standing over me, looking down his massive nose. I'm surprised he can even see past it, to be honest. That thing is huge. He doesn't look like he's buying my bluff, so I need to lift my game a level or two.

"I don't feel right," I say. "Why are there two of everything?"

I risk a glance over towards the double doors, which are now closed. There's a big sign saying *Test in Progress*. Jelly Brain has his arms cuffed behind his back and is sitting on a bench. The guard is sticking some industrial-looking electrodes on his head. The poor kid is about to be wiped clean.

There's a beeping in my ear. I spin my head around and the mind probe nearly takes my nose off. I almost wish I had this security guard's hooter. I could have smashed the probe out of the park. As it is, I just get to stare at the flashing red lights and the smug expression on the security thug's face. I too have been rumbled.

I let go of my head and try to make a dash for it, but Big Nose is quick. He grabs hold of my leg and reels me in like a minnow. If I'd been in my own body I could have put up a fight, but this scrawny kid has less meat on him than a chicken nugget.

The security guard pins me to the ground with just one hand in the middle of my back, my face pressed against the cold floor.

I hear the click-click of cuffs, which surely signifies the end of my little excursion. I know exactly what happens to my host at this point. The depth scanner to establish time and date of first upload, then the temporal erasing, followed by a nice little criminal mind record. Not for me, though. I'm always careful to cover my tracks. The best they'll get out of me is a fake name and an IP address in Guatemala. This kid, however, is a different story. And not one with a happy ending. I should know.

I wonder how things would have turned out if I hadn't tried to cheat on *my* Life Test. I'd probably have got half-decent results. But would that have kept me off the streets, or was I always destined to live this way, ripping people off wherever I can? I feel a slight build-up of acid in my stomach, like I've got indigestion. Or maybe it's something else? Guilt. But it's not like this is my fault. Young

Cedric chose to upload my mind. There's not much I can do to help him now.

And anyway, this kid's probably posh enough to get by without good Life Test results. He'll be fine.

Big Nose has my arms bound behind my back as he leads me over to the bench. The other kid – Joshua – has got all his marbles back. There are suction marks where the electrodes were only moments ago.

"Where am I?" he asks, looking around. The disorientation on his face betrays him as a novice, a first-timer. "What day is it?"

"It's Life Test day!" says Mrs Poodle. "And the test started ten minutes ago! Not that it matters to you now."

Joshua's jaw almost lands in his lap and his eyes glaze over as though they're about to start leaking. Kids these days, honestly. I hope this situation toughens these two up a bit, because without any Life Test results, they're going to need to be a whole lot tougher. Like me.

Big Nose plops me down on the bench next to Joshua.

"How much did you erase?" he asks his security buddy.

"His first upload was eight weeks ago," he says through a smile, "so I scrubbed the last three months."

"I'll make it four, just in case," Big Nose says, attaching the suction pads to my forehead. "There were no upload probes on this one, so he must have covered his tracks well. I'm guessing he's a seasoned Mastermind."

Four months! They're going to erase four months of learning? Any revision he's done is about to be wiped clean. My stomach churns and I suddenly feel a bit queasy. I haven't even been here half an hour and I'd bet my offshore bank balance that this is the first time this kid's ever tampered. It looks like his friend went all jelly brained on him and he tried to help.

What would have happened if I'd had a friend like Cedric when I was their age? Would he have looked out for me? Would it have been enough to keep me off the streets?

"Wait!" I say, unsure what the heck has gotten into me. "That's not fair. Use the depth scanner on me too."

"Sorry, kid," he says, even though he doesn't look remotely sorry. "You should've thought about that before you tried to cheat on your Life Test."

He turns the dial on the control pad in his hand, then moves his fingers towards the erase button.

"No, no, no!" I blurt, unable to stop myself now. "I'm not the kid, I'm a mind hacker. And he didn't cheat … I forced entry so I could rob him!"

Big Nose is staring at me with wide eyes. I have his undivided attention now.

"What's your name, then?" he asks suspiciously, as if he doesn't believe a word I'm saying. Which is hardly surprising. Who ever heard of a mind hacker actually confessing to a crime?

He wants my name. Of course he does. Catching a mind hacker in an innocent child would make him a hero. I can't give it to him, though. I'd be thrown into prison for the rest of my life if they got hold of me.

I take a deep breath and exhale through my nose.

"Kenneth," I say through gritted teeth. "Kenneth Edward Johnson. But my hacker name is Nice Guy Eddie."

Big Nose gulps and exchanges glances with his buddy. They can't quite believe what they are hearing.

"*The* Nice Guy Eddie?"

I nod.

"And where are you projecting from?" he asks. Of course.

159

It's my turn to gulp.

"Before I tell you," I say, feeling my eyes go all glassy, "I want you to change that dial to thirty minutes. And promise me you'll let these kids sit the rest of the test."

I hear Joshua gasp beside me. Even though he just lost the last three months of learning, at least he'll have a chance to do his best. Which is better than no chance at all.

The security guards exchange looks again, then they both nod. Big Nose looks down at the screen in his hands and makes some adjustments.

"Show me!"

When I see it says thirty minutes I close my eyes and take a few deep breaths. This could well be the last free air I breathe in my life. But it's not much of a life, is it? Holed up in a grotty apartment, waiting to jump into unsuspecting bodies so I can rip the owners off. But what else could I have done without sitting my Life Test?

"Apartment 124c, Floor 38, Southside Tower Twelve."

I wait for Big Nose to tap the address into his tablet and run a location check. "Is that it?" he asks, showing me a little blue dot on a map.

"Yes, that's it," I say. "Hurry up and let these kids go, would you?"

"Okay, Nice Guy Eddie," he says eventually. "We're going to put your mind into temporary storage, until your body can be apprehended by the police."

I nod, not wanting to think about the reality of what he just said. It's better to think about these kids completing their Life Tests. Let's face it, my life's not exactly worth fighting for, but theirs have barely started yet.

"Just get on with it!" I say through gritted teeth. "They're losing valuable seconds here."

Big Nose looks me in the eye, his face all serious.

"We'll tell the police you gave yourself up," he says. "That should reduce your sentence."

I give him another nod as his finger moves towards the pad.

Wow … my mind feels like it's just thawed out. I'm sitting on a bench near the double doors to the test room. How did I suddenly get here? Josh is next to me, staring at me with bulging eyes. I glance at my watch and my heart does a triple somersault. We're late. We're seventeen minutes late for our Life Test.

Two security guards are standing in front of us, looking rather happy with themselves.

"Hold still a second," one of them says, then he leans forward and pulls some electrodes off my head that I didn't even know were there.

"Off you go!" the other guy says. "You've still got three hours, forty-five minutes left."

Josh and I instantly stand up.

I can't believe I've missed the start of the Life Test, but my brain is swimming with facts and there's still enough time left to get them down on paper. As we walk towards the double doors Josh whispers, "O.M.G, Cedric. You just had Nice Guy Eddie hack into your brain. And not only that, he turned himself over to the police!"

"Who's Nice Guy Eddie?" I ask. It's not a name I recognise from my months of studying.

As Josh quietly pushes the double doors open, he says, "He's only the most notorious mind-criminal in the country. But you know what... He actually is a nice guy, after all."

That may well be true, but I don't have time to think about it now. I have to pass this test.

Mum was shouting so loudly the speakers of the babysitting console crackled and hissed. But by that point I was too angry to take any notice. Reese is such an idiot. It's like he winds me up on purpose. I was happily playing in my base – the upturned dining table with Mum's bedsheet draped over the legs – when he launched an all-out war. He must have thrown some cushions first to bring down the defences, then he leapt on me, his knobbly elbows jabbing me right in the back.

"Wayne? Reese? You boys had better not be fighting!" Mum's tinny voice screamed.

The sheet covered my face as I spun around and lashed out with my fists. Two of my punches connected and Reese let out an "Ooof", but it wasn't enough to stop him. No way.

He bought his knee up and it caught me right on the bum cheek.

"Owwwww!" I yelled, clutching my bottom with one hand and swinging my other in a wide punch. It smashed into a table leg and pain shot through my hand and wrist.

That made me REALLY mad.

"My finger is on the freeze button," Mum said. "One more sound and I'm pushing it!"

I should have stopped then. I know I should've. But when Reese gets me going like that, I just lose control.

My right hand was still throbbing and my left was clutching my buttock, so I threw my head forwards and clamped down with my teeth.

My nose donked into the side of his head and I could feel something soft and flappy in my mouth. It was an ear! I'd actually caught his ear in my mouth.

Reese let out an almighty yelp.

"Right!" Mum shouted, and the next thing I knew my whole body went rigid.

She actually did it.

She froze us.

"I can't believe you've made me do this again!" Mum hissed. She was using that shouty whisper she thinks the people in her office can't hear. But I'm pretty sure they can. It's more shout than whisper.

Obviously, Reese and I didn't say anything in response. How could we? Mum had us on complete body shutdown. The bedsheet still covered my face, and my mouth was clamped around Reese's ear. There was nothing I could do about it.

"This is the final straw!" Mum went on. "If that house is not completely spotless by the time I get home, I'm going to get Mrs McClaren back."

Please no! Not Drill Sergeant McClaren. She didn't let us do anything, other than homework and educational games. And we were only allowed to eat fruit or chopped-up carrots. We couldn't even have juice. Only water, which she called Cloud Juice, and that's just annoying.

The babysitter console is a million times better. If you point the cameras the other way, you can pretty much do anything you want, as long as you're not too noisy. Before today, Mum had only used the freeze function once, which wasn't my fault either. That idiot Reese started that one by breaking a raw egg on my head.

This was bad, though. If Mum really did get Mrs McClaren back our afternoons would be ruined.

"Did you hear what I said?" Mum asked.

Neither of us replied. How could we? I was sucking an ear-flavoured gobstopper and Reese was using my tongue as an earplug. Not to mention the fact that we were still completely frozen.

"Oh, right!" Mum said, and a loud tapping noise came through the speakers.

"That's strange." Her tinny voice sounded confused. "The freeze button's frozen."

The seconds crawled past. Reese's ear was still in my mouth, a bit of dribble trickling down my cheek.

There were three loud bangs, as though Mum was hitting her phone on her desk.

Suddenly my body drooped and Reese's ear popped out of my mouth.

"Sorry, Mum!" I said, although for some reason no sound came out of my mouth.

Reese said, "Sorry, Mum!" instead. I assumed he didn't want to go back to the dark days of Mrs McClaren either.

"I'm going to be back in twenty minutes. And if that house is not completely spotless by then, you know what will happen."

The background crackle of the speaker died. She was gone. And we had a whole lot of tidying up to do if we wanted to keep our freedom.

I tried to push myself up, but Reese's elbow just dug into my side.

"Get off me, you idiot!" I said. At least the words came out of my mouth. But I hadn't said them in my head.

"Don't call me an idiot, *you* idiot!" I said again, this sentence also popping from my mouth uninvited.

What the heck was happening?

"Reese?" I said, but Reese's lips moved, not mine, and the word came out of his mouth in his voice.

"How are you doing that?" I didn't think the question, but it popped out of my mouth.

Holy moly! Something very strange was going on. I could still see and feel from my own body, but if I moved or spoke, I controlled Reese.

And Reese was in control of me. Everything he said was coming out of my mouth, and I could feel my arms and legs moving all by themselves.

"I don't know what's going on," I said. "It looks like I'm in control of your body and you're in control of mine."

I tried to move my arms up above my head, but it was Reese that squirmed beneath me, his hand swiping across my face.

"This is so weird, Wayne!" Reese said from my mouth, wiggling all my fingers. "How do we make it stop?"

"How the heck should I know?" That was typical of Reese. It was his fault we were in this crazy mess, but he expected me to get us out of it. "Mum's got the remote babysitter app on her phone, so I guess we'll just have to wait for her to get home."

The biggest problem was that I was still underneath Mum's bedsheet, so I couldn't see a thing. Actually, what was I thinking? That definitely wasn't the biggest problem. It just made all the other problems even more problematic.

I lifted my hand to my face to try to get a grip on the sheet.

"Ow!" Reese said. "You just made me poke myself in the eye!"

"Sorry," I said, "but I can't see anything. Can you reach up and pull the sheet away from my face?"

My own hand moved straight up and donked me on the nose. I swear he did that on purpose.

"Stop being a dick!" I said while my own hand swiped at the air around my face, like it was swatting flies away. Eventually he managed to grip the sheet with it.

"You've got it!" I said. "Now lift it up over my head."

"I can't. I'm lying on you," he said. "You need to move me off you if you want to get the sheet off."

I pushed out with my arms and lifted my head back, as though trying to stand up. I felt the weight shift and there was a loud thump.

Without me doing anything, my arm pulled the sheet up and over my head. I could finally see again.

But it wasn't a great sight.

Reese was lying on his back, next to the upturned table. And there was stuff everywhere. Cushions. Sweet wrappers. Juice cartons. Lego blocks.

The place was a complete mess. And if we didn't get it tidied up in the next fifteen minutes, we'd be back on carrot sticks and Cloud Juice every day of the week.

"We've gotta clean all this up," I said, and it was so weird seeing Reese's lips move as the words came from his mouth.

"Make me sit up, would ya? I wanna see how bad it is."

Now that I could see Reese, it was easier for me to move him. I held his arms out, rested his hands on the carpet and pushed his body upright until he was sitting. I then made him turn his head from side to side, so he could take in the whole scene.

"What a nightmare!" he said. "It'd be hard enough cleaning this up normally. It's gonna be totally impossible if I have to control you."

"We'll need to work as a team," I said. "If we make sure we're facing each other at all times, we'll be able to move each other's bodies."

"Okay, let's see if we can both stand up."

I held Reese's arms out for balance and carefully manoeuvred his feet into position, while my own body started to rise. My foot slipped on the edge of the table and I fell forwards, the table leg crashing into my stomach. I lifted my arms up to protect myself, but all that happened was that Reese's arms rose into the air. And my head thumped against the floor.

"Ow!" I said. "Be careful, you idiot. That really hurt."

"Sorry, it was an accident!"

He tried again, more slowly this time, and I could feel myself rising until I was on my feet.

"Keep my arms out for balance," I said. "I don't want to fall over again."

"Okay, but we need to be quicker than this if we're gonna get this whole place tidy before Mum gets home."

He had a point.

"Let's start with the table," I said. "If we grab an end each, we should be able to turn it the right way up."

That is actually much more difficult than it sounds. Just getting us lined up so we were both facing the table took ages. Then we leaned each other forward and tried to grab the edge. It's hard enough sliding your own fingers underneath something to lift it up. It's nearly impossible when you're controlling someone else's hands.

As we lifted it up, one of the table legs almost went up my nose.

"Careful," I said. "Turn it now!"

I twisted the table, hoping to spin it around. But Reese made me turn the other way and we dropped it.

"Arrrggghhhh!" Reese screamed. "That landed on my foot."

His reflexes made my foot shoot backwards. I toppled over, my forehead crashing into the middle of the table. Bright white dots speckled my vision as I lay there, cold wood pressing against my cheek.

This was not going well.

"We'll have to try that again," I said. "But keep your voice down. If Mum gets another volume alert she'll turn her video on, and then we'll be in trouble."

We carefully got ourselves on either side of the table again, and this time, we both turned it the same direction. We even moved our heads back so that neither of us got a table leg up the nose. We were getting better at this.

"What should we do next?" Reese asked, once the table was where it should be.

"Let's take the sheet back to Mum's bed," I said.

"Get lost. We've just tidied up some of your mess," Reese said, turning my face into a scowl. "Let's do some of mine now."

Tom E. Moffatt

I didn't say anything. We needed to work together and getting into another argument wouldn't speed things up.

"Let's put the Lego away," he said, moving me over to the mountain of Lego blocks in the middle of the living room.

"Okay, but turn my head so I can see you."

I carefully manoeuvred Reese's body across the room, using the furniture for support. It wasn't easy though, especially while my own body was jerking along at the same time. It was like trying to run a three-legged race while blindfolded. With someone who really annoys you.

"Ow, you idiot," Reese said. "You just made me step on a piece of Lego."

"You shouldn't have made such a mess then, should you?"

We sat each other down next to the empty Lego box and began putting all the pieces back in, one or two at a time. It took ages.

I turned Reese's head towards the clock on the baby-sitting unit. "What time is it?" I asked.

"We've only got eight minutes until Mum's due home. But if you keep making me look in the opposite direction, it'll take a lot longer than that!"

I faced him back towards me and made him pick up several blocks at once, while my own hand grabbed one of the large green bases and used it to scoop up some smaller pieces. It took a lot of concentration, and for a moment the only sound was the clicking of the Lego pieces landing in the box.

"Let's do that sheet now," I said, once the last of the blocks had been cleared away.

"Why don't you make me do it, while I make you tidy up the rest of the rubbish here?" Reese asked.

As you can see, my brother is not that bright.

"Great idea, genius!" I said. "We need to see each other, or we'll both end up walking into walls. Plus it will be much easier to get it back on Mum's bed with two of us."

"Okay, hurry. Mum'll be home any minute."

Sometimes you actually get things done quicker if you do them slowly. I know that sounds illogical, but it's true. Whenever Mum tries to do the shopping in a hurry she ends up forgetting half the things she needs and has to go back to the supermarket the next day, which takes her way longer than if she'd taken her time in the first place.

This was a bit like that. Reese made me rush towards the sheet at full speed, but he lost my balance and I fell forward, landing right on top of it. That got my legs tangled in the sheet and I had to move his body closer to unwrap me.

By the time we made it to Mum's room and shoved the sheet back on the bed, twenty-three minutes had passed. She could walk through the front door at any moment and the living room still had empty wrappers and cushions strewn across the floor, like a typhoon had hit.

"Quick," Reese said. "I think I just heard a car pull up!"

We both rushed each other into the living room and threw the cushions back onto the couch, until there were only sweet wrappers and juice cartons on the floor.

I made Reese crouch down – since it was easier to balance that way – then grabbed three juice cartons. A car door slammed in the driveway as Reese picked up the rest of the stuff.

"Where do I put them?" Reese demanded frantically. He swiped at my pocket with a handful of wrappers but couldn't get them in with one hand. I moved his body over towards the couch, planning to hide them under a cushion. But Reese had other ideas. He pulled at the waistband of my trousers and stuffed the wrappers inside my pants.

"Oi, don't be an idiot!" I shouted. "That's gross!"

"Stop being a wuss! It's better than having Mrs McClaren babysit us for the rest of our lives."

"Fine," I said, stopping Reese and grabbing his own waistband. I quickly made him stuff the empty drink cartons inside his own underpants.

"Wait! That's not fair! They're way bigger," he said, walking me over towards him. I really hoped he didn't plan on using my hand to grab the cartons out of his undies.

I moved him backwards to get his body out of the way, but walking backwards was even harder than going forwards. His foot caught the corner of the couch and he toppled over. I totally forgot to put his arms up to protect him and his head crashed onto the floor with a loud thud.

"You're gonna pay for that!" he said, walking me over to his body. Then he stopped, clearly unsure what to do next. His normal approach would have been to punch me, but that would have meant punching himself.

My expression suddenly changed into a smile, and I could tell that Reese had just come to the same conclusion. My own arm rose into the air and my fist clenched into a ball.

"No, Reese. Don't!" I said, as keys jangled in the door.

Even that didn't stop him.

Bam!

He made me punch myself right in the nose. And once wasn't enough, even. He did another two whacks to my face, then made me punch myself in the stomach.

My brother's a lunatic. He really is.

I thought about making him hit himself, but it feels wrong punching yourself as hard as you can in the face. Even if it actually hurts someone else.

Instead, I reached Reese's arm out and yanked at my own leg, so I fell on top of him. I then made Reese grab my arm, so he couldn't do any more damage.

"What do you two think you're doing?" Mum asked in that shouty kind of way that isn't actually a question.

Reese didn't even stop at that. He'd gone completely mental and was still trying to make me punch myself in the face. Fortunately, we were now piled on the floor and I had hold of his arms, so he couldn't get a proper swing. But there was already blood trickling out of my nose and Reese wasn't close to stopping.

He shook my arm free and was just about to take another swing at my nose when we both froze.

"I can't believe you made me use the freeze button twice in one day! That is absolutely disgraceful!" Mum's face was all scrunched up and there were bits of spit flying out of her mouth as she spoke.

Neither of us said anything in return. Obviously. In fact, I think that's what sold Mum on the babysitting unit in the first place. The fact that she had the power to stop us answering back.

"That's it, then. You clearly can't be trusted on your own. I'm sending this ridiculous babysitting device back and asking Mrs McClaren to look after you again."

I tried to let out a groan but my body was still on lockdown.

We'd failed. We got so close, and then my stupid brother ruined it.

"I want you to apologise to each other, then go to your rooms for some thinking time."

Then Mum must have pressed the button, because our muscles suddenly relaxed and we could move again. Thank goodness!

Reese clenched his fist into a ball and punched himself in the nose as hard as he could. His own nose! A little trickle of blood crept out of his nostril and I couldn't help laughing.

"I saw that, young man! Don't think you can get Wayne in trouble by making it look like he hit you, too. You are grounded for an entire month!"

"What about me?" I asked, happy that the question came from my own lips, even though they were swollen and covered in blood from my leaking nose.

"You're grounded for one week." Which wasn't all that bad, considering. At least I'd get three glorious weeks where I could wind Reese up every day.

"And I am phoning Mrs McClaren this instant."

She fiddled with her phone as Reese and I untangled ourselves miserably.

"This is your fault!" Reese hissed, jabbing me in the ribs while Mum wasn't looking.

I took myself off to my room before he could hit me again. Thinking about it now, perhaps having Drill Sergeant McClaren might not be so bad. She's the only person who can keep Reese under control.

Reuben can remember the exact moment he heard about the feet. Most people can. It was May 12, 2027, the morning after they appeared. He was sitting in the kitchen at the pop-up counter, eating a bowl of Nutriflakes. Dad was standing beside him in his overalls, buttering some toasted croissants.

Mum walked into the kitchen in her dressing gown and slippers, holding the news tablet out in front of her. She let out a gasp and stopped in the middle of the room, her eyes scanning the screen. Her face was pale and worry lines stood out on her forehead.

"What's wrong?" Dad asked, walking over to Mum and reading over her shoulder.

"Oh no," he said, wincing. "That is so sick."

"What is it?" Reuben asked. "What's happened?"

It looked like someone important must have died. Or another war broken out. Reuben placed his spoon on the counter and braced himself for bad news. Mum and Dad glanced at each other, as if deciding whether or not to tell him.

"They found a pair of feet," Dad said slowly. "In the centre of Cambridge."

"It looks like they belonged to a child," Mum said, looking down at the ground.

They wouldn't tell him much more than that, but as soon as Reuben arrived at school he found out exactly what had happened. It was all anyone was talking about.

At 18:45 on Tuesday 11 May, a pair of feet had been discovered standing in the middle of the street. They were wearing trainers with odd socks and had been amputated about three inches below the knees.

No one saw anyone leaving them there, but there was a minor collision as an autocar swerved, crashing into two unmanned delivery vehicles.

One eyewitness, a homeless man named Ding Klopper, claimed that they'd appeared out of mid-air and caused the accident, but police suspected he'd been drinking. All other eyewitnesses reported seeing the feet moments later, standing in the middle of the road next to the crash scene.

Police searched the area for clues, then the feet were taken to a medical facility to be analysed by a team of scientists. They were believed to belong to a boy of eleven or twelve years of age and appeared to have been surgically removed, perhaps with laser technology, while the boy was still alive.

That was what intrigued Reuben so much. Somewhere out there was a boy, only a year or so older than him, missing a pair of feet. Some people suspected that he might have died since the operation, but Reuben was convinced he was still alive. He could feel it in his gut.

In the days and weeks that followed there were daily broadcasts and announcements, appealing to whoever was holding the boy. The feet had been stored on ice and could be reattached, if only the owner were known, but there was absolutely no sign of him.

There was even a fifty thousand dollar reward for any information that led to the boy's whereabouts, which made Reuben completely obsessed. That kind of money would totally solve his family's financial troubles. Mum wouldn't have to work so much. Dad could spend less time in his workshop. If only he could solve the mystery.

Reuben began to act like a private detective, scouring the internet at every opportunity. He searched for clues and theories, and discussed them with friends and family.

Everyone had an opinion.

His mum thought they might belong to an illegal immigrant. Someone who could be deported if they came forward.

Dad blamed an underground organ donation racket.

Reuben's best friend, Dai, thought the boy had been hit by a truck going so fast that his body had been vaporised. But no one had seen a truck. And no one had been reported missing.

It was all speculation.

After a few months, the news stopped reporting anything at all. Reuben set his web-analyser to alert him if the feet were mentioned, but if they were, it was usually other Misfeets, as such enthusiasts were known, discussing various theories.

Six months later, an article came through on his analyser, announcing that the feet were going on display in the National Museum's Mysteries exhibit. Reuben just had to see them. He begged his parents. He did chores around the house. He even offered to pay the travel costs out of his own pocket money.

Eventually, Mum agreed to take him.

His dad was too busy in his workshop, as always, but Reuben and his mum caught a bus into town. The polished floors of the National Museum were unaccustomed to so much foot traffic. People had come from all over the country to queue up to see the feet. Reuben stood in line with his mum for two hours, his own feet aching and restless, before they arrived at the refrigerated glass cabinet.

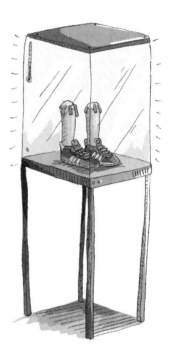

After all that, the feet didn't even look that special. The top parts, where they had been amputated, were covered in medical cream and tape, in case the owner ever came forward. The skin was smooth and pale, just like the feet of any eleven-year-old boy. Reuben thought they looked just like his own feet, although you'd never catch him wearing odd socks.

The trainers were pretty cool, though. They were black Adidas with three yellow stripes and yellow laces. They looked like bumblebees. Loads of kids at school had already bought the same shoes, and straight after the visit Reuben started dragging his feet on the walk to and from school.

"Your trainers are looking rather worn," Mum said one Saturday a few weeks later. "We'll pop into town today to get you some new ones."

Reuben suppressed a smile and then offered to help clear the breakfast dishes away.

"Are you going to come with us, Dad?" he asked, while carrying his empty bowl to the sink. Dad was a bit of a pushover. If he came Reuben would definitely get the bumblebee trainers.

"I'd love to, Reuben," Dad said. "I really would. But I've got to keep working on my invention. I'm getting so close."

Reuben should have known better. Dad was always busy. It had been stupid to think he might come.

It didn't matter, though. He made sure he was extra chatty on the way into town, asking Mum questions about when she was little and carrying the shopping bags for her.

Then, when they were in the shoe shop, he pointed to the bumblebee shoes.

"Can I have those?"

"Aren't they the same ones the feet were wearing?" Mum said, her eyebrows raised. "Really? You want those?"

Reuben nodded.

Next thing he knew, he was walking out of the shop wearing a brand-new pair of bumblebee trainers. They were the coolest things ever.

A few months after that, Dad finally finished his invention. Reuben had never seen him so excited. He came into the living room while Mum and Reuben were playing Scrabble. He couldn't stand still, leaping from foot to foot, his eyes lit up like sparklers.

"It works! It actually works!" he said.

Mum's mouth fell open.

"You've tried it? And it actually works?"

Dad nodded, his smile taking over his whole face. "Come and see. I'll show you."

They jumped up and raced to his workshop, giggling and pushing each other out of the way like excited little kids. Reuben got there first, skidding to a halt at the workshop door. He gripped the handle and yanked it open, anticipation fluttering around his stomach like a flock of birds.

Over the years, Reuben's dad had come up with some pretty cool inventions. But he always aimed high, so there had also been quite a few failures. When he'd said he was working on a time machine, Reuben had expected this to be one of those failures. After all, thousands of people throughout history had tried to make time machines, but no one had even come close. Except in the movies, of course.

His dad's time machine didn't look like much. In fact, it resembled a metal teepee. Thick steel bars all came together in a point at the top and

sheets of metal filled all the gaps. A screen and a control panel sat next to an oval door, which looked like it belonged on an early spacecraft.

Dad tapped away on a keyboard, until an image of their back garden appeared on his computer screen. A sparrow hopped around in the middle of the overgrown lawn, pecking at the ground.

"This shows us last Tuesday at ten in the morning," Dad said, stepping away from his desk and rubbing his hands together. "We just need my trusty test pilot to go back in time."

He glanced over at the cat, who was asleep on an armchair. "Tosca, are you ready to boldly go where no cat has gone before?" Dad said, as he strolled towards her. The poor cat yawned and stretched as he picked her up and carried her towards the machine.

"Wouldn't it be better to try it out on something less alive first?" Mum asked. "Like a cactus or a lump of cheese?"

"Don't worry, dear," Dad said. "All the preliminary tests have worked just fine. This will be Tosca's third trip, and she didn't even wake up on the last two."

He placed the cat down in the middle of the machine and closed the door. Through the glass window next to the control panel Reuben could see Tosca looking up at them with her dark eyes.

Dad pulled up an image on the screen that looked like Google Maps.

"Now I need to select our back garden as the location," he said, zooming in on our house, "so we can catch it on camera."

A map of their garden filled the screen and Dad double-tapped his finger in the middle. A small pin appeared, along with the words, *Select date and time.*

Dad selected last Tuesday at 10:03 a.m. from the dropdown calendar, then he tapped several more buttons until the screen displayed the words *Commence Countdown.*

"You press it, Reuben," he said, taking a step backwards.

Reuben looked through the window. Tosca had stretched out on her side and resumed her afternoon nap. Reuben tapped the button and the screen filled with numbers.

10, 9, 8…

A loud hum filled the room, but Tosca didn't even open her eyes.

7, 6, 5, 4…

Reuben felt a tug on his T-shirt and realised that his parents had both stepped away from the time machine. Mum had her back up against the wall, and her worried frown showed that she'd rather be even further away. He quickly joined them, his breath rasping through his nose.

3, 2, 1…

As the hum reached its crescendo, a flash of red light lit up the windows of the time machine. Reuben glanced up and saw that Mum had her eyes closed.

When he looked back at the time machine, it was gone. Vanished. Instead, he found himself staring at a rusty saw hanging from a nail on the far wall of the workshop.

"Woah!" he said, breaking the fresh silence. "Where did it go?"

Dad turned around with an enormous smile on his face. "I'll show you where it went. And *when* it went. Look!"

He pointed towards his computer screen, which still showed their back garden last Tuesday. But now there was a large metal teepee in the centre of it.

"I can't believe it," Mum said, rubbing her eyes as she took a few steps forward. "You've done it! You've actually done it."

"I have," Dad said through a wide grin. "But I wouldn't go much closer if I were you... two tonnes of metal will be back at any second."

They all stared in silence at the far wall of the workshop for a moment, until the time machine appeared out of nowhere, humming faintly.

When Reuben peered in through its window, he could just make out the sleeping form of Tosca through a light fog. The cat was still curled up on her side, her face tucked into her paw.

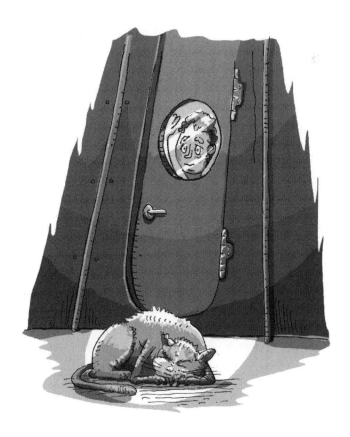

Now Reuben was impressed. In fact, he couldn't believe it. His dad – his own father – had created a time-travelling machine!

"What do you think?" Dad said, rubbing his hands together as though trying to warm them up. "You can programme it to go anywhere in the world. At any time in history. Just think of all the amazing events we can witness first-hand. The mysteries we'll be able to solve!"

Reuben's jaw nearly hit the ground. This was incredible. It was the best thing ever. Imagine all the places they could visit. The things they could discover.

Then a thought pounced into his mind.

He could find out how the feet got there! Using the time machine, he could go to the centre of Cambridge at that exact moment and see who left them. He'd be famous. And he'd get the fifty thousand dollar reward.

Reuben was so excited he couldn't contain himself. But he didn't want to let his parents know what he was planning, just in case they tried to stop him.

"I haven't experimented with any larger objects yet," Dad said, "but all my initial tests have been completely successful. I should be ready to announce it to the world within a few weeks."

That was awesome and he was happy for his dad. But first Reuben wanted to figure out how the feet had got there. Before everyone knew they had a time machine.

When he got into bed that night, he was wide awake with excitement. His mind was spinning with the possibilities of what he might see. Would he witness an accident? Or catch a criminal in action? Or maybe he was about to uncover a whole truckload of body parts. Perhaps they'd give him more than fifty thousand dollar. He might get a million dollars.

Once the house was quiet, he sneaked out of bed. He fumbled around in the dark for the T-shirt and shorts he'd left lying on the floor, then grabbed the first two socks he could find in his underwear drawer. He put his bumblebee trainers on and pocketed his smartphone, so he could take photos of whatever he discovered.

Reuben opened the door very slowly and tiptoed out of his room. Moonlight shone through the net curtains as he carefully stepped over the creaky floorboards in the hallway and crept down the stairs.

It wasn't long before he was closing the workshop door behind

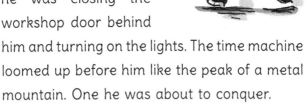

him and turning on the lights. The time machine loomed up before him like the peak of a metal mountain. One he was about to conquer.

When he pressed the power button there was a faint whir, like a computer starting up. The screen flickered to life and Reuben stared at it, trying to remember what Dad had done. Eventually he saw the location button, then zoomed in on the map until he found

Cambridge town centre. He tapped a spot close to where he thought the feet had been discovered. The date and time part was easy. Everyone knew that. He selected 11 May at 06:45 p.m. from the dropdown menu.

It was the next step he wasn't sure about. Where was the countdown button? He remembered pushing it last time, right in the middle of the screen. But where was it now?

He stared at all the dials and labels, not sure which ones to press.

GPS Alignment

Power Signature Stabilisation

Chronometer Adjustment

Why couldn't Dad use words that made sense?

Reuben took a deep breath through his nose. He'd come this far. There was no way he was going to give up now. He held out his index finger and jabbed two, three, four buttons.

The *Commence Countdown* button popped onto the screen and Reuben let out a big puff of air, his heart pounding in his ears. Yes! This was it. The moment of truth. The whole world was about to know how those feet got there.

Reuben held his finger out again and time seemed to slow as he moved it forward and pressed the big red button.

The deep hum filled the room.

10, 9, 8...

He swung the door open and rushed inside the machine, the sound vibrating through his bones like the bassline at a rock concert.

7, 6, 5...

Reuben pulled the door shut behind him as the sound changed from a hum into a horrible clunking, like bits of metal being sucked up a vacuum cleaner. It was so loud his teeth rattled in his jaw.

4, 3, 2...

A twisty, churny feeling filled his stomach as he held his breath and glanced at the door. Maybe this wasn't such a good idea!

1...

The machine filled with a thick mist and red light flickered all around him, illuminating his trainers and rising up his legs. There was a sudden flash of light and pain. Reuben fell to the floor.

As the red light faded and the mist cleared, he could still see the roof of the workshop through the glass panel. Why was he not in Cambridge? And why was he lying on the floor?

Reuben tried to sit up, but he fell back to the ground. There was still red all around him. But it wasn't light. It was deep, dark red. It was blood.

That was when he noticed that his feet were missing. They were gone. Cut clean off at his shins. And his blood was leaking out over the floor of the time machine. He stretched his arm towards the door handle, but it was too far away. He couldn't reach it.

Panic reared up inside him like a monster trying to escape. He was losing so much blood. If he didn't get to hospital soon, he would die. He reached into his pocket and pulled out his blood-soaked phone. His hands shook and his vision blurred as he selected his home phone number.

His mum's sleepy voice cut in after two rings.

"Hello? Who is this?"

Reuben fought to keep his eyes open.

"Mum! In the time machine… Help!"

And then he passed out.

The next thing Reuben knew, he was lying in a hospital bed. Bright light streamed through the window, making the white walls glow. There was no one around, but he could hear the bustle of a busy hospital on the other side of the door. A vase of wilting flowers sat on the bedside table, surrounded by tons of *Get Well Soon* cards, so he must have been here a while.

But why was he even in hospital? And where were his parents?

That thought brought everything flooding back to him. The time machine. His feet. He'd lost his feet!

Reuben looked down the length of the bed and saw two bumps underneath the sheets

exactly where his feet should be. He wiggled his toes and both the bumps moved. He was okay. His feet were back. Lifting the bedsheets up, he examined them more closely. His shins were wrapped in bandages, but his feet looked and felt completely normal.

"Oh, you're awake!" a voice said, and Reuben looked up to see a nurse standing in the doorway. "And I see you can wiggle your toes. That's fantastic news."

Reuben smiled, not really knowing what to say.

"You must be famished. Have a bite to eat while I fetch your parents." She pointed at a covered plate on the tray table next to his bed, then marched off down the corridor.

Reuben *was* quite hungry for food, but he was even hungrier for information. And he'd just spotted his phone next to the plate.

He turned it on and clicked straight into his web-analyser. There were more than five thousand alerts. The whole world was talking about the feet. About his feet!

He scrolled through some of the headlines:

Foot Mystery Finally Solved

Museum Feet Save Boy's Life

Time-Travelling by Foot

Suddenly everything made perfect sense. They had been his feet all along. Dad's time machine had sent them to Cambridge from the future. Reuben was the missing boy everyone had been looking for.

And now he was famous. His face was in newspapers and on TV screens all over the world. He didn't get the fifty thousand dollar reward, though. That had gone to the paramedics who'd saved his life, which Reuben had to admit was fair.

But his family still needed money. Especially now that there'd be hospital bills on top of everything else.

Reuben scrolled through the news feed on his phone, looking at all the pictures of him and his feet. The reporters were desperate to interview him, so maybe he'd get paid for that. But would it be enough?

A slow smile spread across Reuben's face as a thought came to him. He searched Google for a phone number, then gave it a call.

"Hi, is that Adidas? This is Reuben Walker. I'd like to talk about a possible sponsorship deal..."

"I really hope you're not going to cause a scene, young lady," Mum said, holding the car door open.

Priscilla closed her eyes and tightened her grip on the headrest. Maybe she *should* cause a scene. Maybe she should run into Mum's workplace, screaming as loud as she could. Smashing everything she saw. Then the police would be called and they'd be kept on Earth to be punished. Some other family would have to go to that stupid rock halfway across the solar system.

Mum folded her arms and took a deep breath through her nose. "If I'm late for the handover meeting I am going to be furious."

"And if I don't get to eat at least eight chocolate eclairs, I'll be even hangrier!" Dad said, rubbing his rather large tummy.

Priscilla tried not to smile. Dad was annoying like that. He always said something silly that made it hard to stay upset.

"Wow," Felicity said. She was standing on the pavement, clutching Noddy and staring up at the LMC building. "It's big like a volcano!"

"Your sister's only five years old, and she's coming along without a fuss," Mum said, glancing at the time on her phone.

"That's cos she hasn't got any friends yet. It's totally fine for her. She doesn't know any better." As she spoke, Priscilla glanced at the building. It was rather impressive. She couldn't see much of it from the car, but the thin silanium towers shot off at crazy angles that normal metals just couldn't achieve.

At that moment the huge doors slid open, revealing Professor Inks. She was wearing a pristine three-piece suit and looked more like she was going to an interview than a boring old handover meeting.

"Welcome, welcome," she said, her arms spread wide as though she was coming in for a group cuddle. "On behalf of the Lunar Mining Corporation, I would just like to say how happy we are that you are all here, ready to embark on this exciting journey."

Mum glared into the car, her no-nonsense expression making Priscilla release her grip on the headrest. She stepped out of the vehicle and walked towards Professor Inks. She wasn't going to smile, though. No way.

"Here comes our happy little adventurer," Dad said, hanging onto Goliath's lead. "She's nearly as excited as the dog is."

Goliath was panting profusely as he pulled Dad towards the entrance. If only the stupid dog knew what he'd been signed up for. He'd be yanking Dad in the opposite direction!

As Dad and Goliath whooshed into the lobby, Priscilla turned to stare at their car as it drove off on auto. One more thing that she wouldn't see for three whole years.

"That's the spirit, Malcolm," Professor Inks said as she struggled to keep up with Dad. "We do need to hurry. The Singhs are already out of stasis."

Priscilla's eyes widened as they entered the debrief room. A long table lining the far wall was piled high with every type of food you could imagine. There were pies and lobsters and pineapples and lollies. Someone had even had the foresight to fill a large trough with dog food.

Once Goliath spotted that, Dad gave up trying to contain him. He let go of the lead and Goliath crossed the room in three strides before burying his head deep in the food.

"Now that the dog's taken care of, where are those eclairs?" Dad asked, rubbing his hands together as he sauntered over to the sweet end of the table.

The other family, the Singhs, were already seated. They each had a plate of food piled high in front of them and were devouring it like they hadn't eaten in three years.

Priscilla had planned on sulking in the corner, but curiosity was getting the better of her. She wanted to speak to the Singh girl to find out what life was like on Ganymede, Jupiter's largest moon. And while she was at it, she might as well enjoy some of this food. She grabbed a plate and walked the length of the table, trying to figure out what to go for. Dad had found his eclairs and was making his plate look like a Jenga tower. Mum and Felicity had both headed straight for the sushi, but Priscilla just couldn't decide. It all looked so good.

By the third lap, all she had selected was a slice of Hawaiian pizza. Everyone else was already seated.

She thought about trying to attract Mum's attention, to get a bit of help, but she was deep in conversation with Mr Singh.

Fortunately, Professor Inks came to her rescue.

"Having trouble deciding, are we?"

Priscilla nodded.

"It can be rather overwhelming when there are so many options. I tend to go for quality over quantity. Take a tiny piece of everything that looks tasty. You can always come back for more of the best ones later."

Priscilla glanced along the length of the table again. It did have some delicious-looking stuff.

She started at one end and moved slowly along, grabbing one of everything that she fancied. A shrimp. A vol-au-vent. A slice of quiche. A giant strawberry. A chocolate eclair, before Dad ate them all.

By the time she reached the far end, she'd piled her plate high with food. Professor Inks gave her a wink as she made her way over to the table and sat down beside Felicity, whose hands and face already looked like they had been dipped in chocolate.

At the other end of the table, Mr Singh was talking loudly, waving a crab's pincer around for emphasis.

"...not had a single issue in three years, other than the occasional minor moonquake!" he said, before sucking juice out of the crab's arm. "It was a dream placement."

"If you like being bored out of your mind!" the daughter, Dina, whispered to Priscilla. She had her phone out and was scrolling through messages with one hand while popping entire pieces of sushi into her mouth with the other.

Priscilla put down the slice of salami she'd been about to eat, her curiosity overtaking her hunger.

"Really?" she asked. "Is it that bad?"

Dina nodded, her eyes narrowing. "Yeah. The living quarters are tiny. There's no internet and the teacher-bot is so annoying. It just makes you work in silence for six hours a day."

Priscilla's chest tightened as the anger welled up inside her again. She'd known it was going to be bad, but that sounded absolutely awful.

"But the worst part is having to live in a different body for three years. It's so gross. Hopefully, you'll be in my clone. It's a tall female with pale skin and fair hair. Or perhaps you'll get the male. One of you will have to take the male clone since the second female won't be ready for months."

Dina's voice softened at the horrified look on Priscilla's face. "The only thing that makes it remotely bearable is the Garden Pod. It's filled with tropical plants and bird life, and there are loads of treehouses and dens to explore. It just about kept me sane."

Priscilla popped the strawberry into her mouth and exhaled through her nose. Six hours of silent schoolwork a day? No internet? A male body? Only having a silly little garden to play in? This was going to be an absolute nightmare.

"And don't expect nice food like this," Dina said, pointing at the remaining sushi on her plate. "You'll be living on bland space slop for the next three years."

Priscilla closed her eyes, hoping that would be enough to stop the tears from pouring out.

The launch room was even more impressive than the outside of the building, but Priscilla barely glanced at it. She hadn't said a word through the rest of the handover lunch. And she didn't even want to look at her parents in the lift on the way up to the top floor. This was all Mum's fault. Why did she have to accept this stupid placement? If she'd said no, the Lunar

Mining Corporation would have found some other engineer to go. Her family could have stayed in their lovely house. Priscilla could have carried on at school, hanging out with all her friends.

She was already strapped into her transmission seat by the time she took a good look around. Mum, Dad and Felicity were in seats surrounding her, all facing towards the centre of the room. Goliath was squished into a glass tank that barely contained his

enormous body. He was clearly the biggest pet they'd ever had to transmit into space.

The room itself was round, like the inside of a lighthouse. Priscilla knew from previous conversations that the tip of the LMC building was directly above them. Huge funnels hung over their heads, one for each living thing whose mind needed to be transmitted. It was like sitting underneath the jets of a space rocket.

Any moment now the rocket would fire up, but no one would move. At least, nothing solid. Instead, their minds would be blasted across the solar system into the receiver room on Ganymede, where the empty clone bodies were waiting.

Mum smiled at Priscilla, tilting her head to the side, as though to say she was sorry they had to go through this. But she couldn't have been that sorry. Or she wouldn't be making them do it.

Priscilla held her Mum's gaze but did not smile. She didn't want her to think she was remotely happy about this. She glanced at Dad, who went cross-eyed and touched his nose with the tip of his tongue. But not even that made Priscilla smile today. There was nothing funny about this situation.

Technicians hurried around them, checking dials and fastening safety belts. One by one they slipped out of the room until just the Freeman family remained. The lights dimmed and a voice boomed over the speakers.

"READY TO TRANSMIT IN TEN..."

Priscilla couldn't believe these were the last moments in her own body for the next three years.

"NINE, EIGHT, SEVEN..."

Tears formed in her eyes as she gripped the armrest, her fingers digging into the soft material.

"SIX, FIVE, FOUR..."

How could this be happening? She didn't want to be blasted to the other side of the solar system. Or be stuck in a strange body. This was so unfair!

"THREE, TWO, ONE…"

Priscilla closed her eyes and tears trickled down her cheek. She took a deep breath as her chair vibrated.

A low drone filled Priscilla's ears for several seconds as the vibrations intensified . Then nothing.

Priscilla couldn't see, feel or hear anything at all. She was all alone in absolute nothingness. It wasn't even dark. It was just nothing. No body. No place. No movement. Just a faint awareness of existence.

The feeling stretched on as her mind zoomed through space.

Time played tricks on her, too. Priscilla knew that even at this point in space and time, with Ganymede at its closest to Earth, the journey would take thirty-eight minutes. Yet there only seemed to be one elongated moment of nothingness.

Then *BAM!*

Hundreds of sensations hit her all at once. The first was pain. Straps dug into her shoulder blades and neck.

The sound was the next thing. A deafening wail like a siren. And red light. A flashing red light. Like there was some kind of emergency.

Priscilla looked around, disorientated, fear rising up from the pit of her stomach. What was going on?

In the flashes of red she could see the panicked faces of three clones sitting opposite her. Even in the gloomy light they looked pale and sterile. The younger clones, a male and a female, clutched at their safety straps, their eyes glancing around the room. The older male clone gnawed at his straps, his eyes wide and manic.

Priscilla had no idea what was going on. The ear-piercing siren filled her mind, smothering her thoughts.

For some reason, the room was at an angle, as though it had tipped over. Her chair was leaning forwards causing the straps to take all her weight. There were several chairs and boxes piled up on one side of the room. One of the boxes was spinning and wriggling, as though something inside was trying to get free.

"What's happening, Mummy?" the young male clone asked in the lull of the siren.

The question was aimed at Priscilla.

Priscilla stared around the red gloom. She had no idea what was going on, but it was clearly some kind of emergency. Something had gone very wrong.

The fact that they were in clone bodies meant they had made it to Ganymede's moon base. But what were these sirens about? And why was the transmission room on such an angle?

"Something's gone terribly wrong!" shouted the young female clone. "Ella, what's the situation?"

She also aimed the question at Priscilla. A high-pitched bark came from a glass container next to the transmission chairs. Priscilla glanced over to see a small, yappy dog. Only a tenth of the size of Goliath's normal body.

Priscilla let go of the straps she'd been gripping and stared at her hands in the flashing red light. They were adult female hands. She'd been sent into the wrong body.

"I'm not Mum," she said. "It's me. Priscilla."

"Well, I'm Dad," said the young female clone.

"And I'm Felicity," said the young male.

Now that Priscilla's eyes and ears had adjusted to the flashing red light and wailing siren, it was easier to make out what was going on.

"Is that you, Mum?" Priscilla asked the older male clone. His eyes darted between them and his mouth opened, but he didn't answer. He leaned forward and started gnawing at his wrist strap again.

"Where's Mummy?" the boy clone asked, sounding like he was about to cry.

The small dog barked again, looking up at them intently. Then it lifted its left paw and waved at them.

Priscilla stared at the little dog as the answer

clicked into place. Oh no! They really were in a muddle. Somehow she had ended up in the female adult clone, where Mum was supposed to be. Dad was in the girl clone, and Felicity was in the boy clone. Mum was in the dog's body and Goliath was in the adult male clone.

How on Earth – or Ganymede – were they going to get out of this mess?

On the lower side of the room a chair was swept aside, and a small droid spun itself around so its wide feet touched the sloping floor. Slowly and steadily the droid manoeuvred up the steep slope, coming to a halt next to Priscilla.

The droid extended its arm, flashing another red light in Priscilla's eyes as it scanned her face.

"C7219 – Ella Freeman," it said in an expressionless voice. It lowered its arm and spoke again. "I am D362. An emergency situation…"

"I'm not Ella," Priscilla interrupted. "I am Priscilla Freeman. I've been transferred into the wrong body."

The building shook, sending a space helmet clattering off into the lower corner. Priscilla gripped the straps to keep herself level. The antenna on the droid's head wobbled in the moonquake, but its feet stayed firmly attached to the floor. They probably had suction pads or magnets.

The droid's arm extended again and scanned Priscilla's face once more.

"C7219 – Ella Freeman," it repeated. "Identified. An emergency situation has occurred. A moonquake in the north-western quadrant

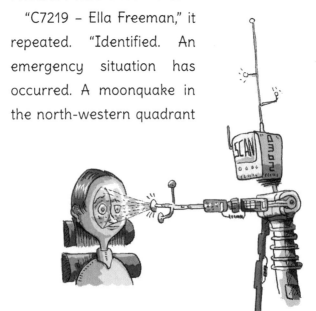

234

has caused irreparable damage. Immediate action required."

Priscilla stared at the other clones, hoping they would help to explain. Out of habit she first turned to the adult clone, but his tongue was hanging out and he was panting. She looked at the two younger clones instead, her eyes settling on the female one.

"What should I do, Dad?" It felt strange calling a pale ten-year-old girl 'Dad'.

"Jeez, I don't know. This is your mother's department." He glanced at the small dog that was looking up at them attentively. "I guess you'll have to go with the robot and see what you can do."

The droid had already turned and was making its way to the closest exit door, its body jutting out at a right angle from the tilted floor. The clunks of its feet kept rhythm with the siren.

Priscilla gripped hold of the chair with one hand and undid the safety belt with the other. As soon as the harness clicked off, she had to hug the back of the chair to stop herself slipping down to the lower side of the room.

She clambered from her seat to the next one, where the older male clone was sitting. Goliath got very excited and licked Priscilla's face, which made it difficult to hang on. The droid was already at the door, so Priscilla lunged for the next seat. Felicity leaned back as far as she could, as Priscilla sized up what to do. There was a three-metre gap between this chair and the door.

If she jumped, she'd probably slide down the floor and end up in a heap at the bottom. But what other choice did she have? She certainly didn't have gripping feet like the droid.

That was it! She could use the droid. After all, this clone was supposed to be in charge of the moon base. The droid would have to do what she told it.

"Droid," she called out, trying to remember its name. Then she spotted black letters on its back. "D362, move towards me."

The droid obeyed, its feet gripping the sloping metal floor as it clunked its way back.

"Stop," she called, once D362 was less than a metre away. There was another lurch and the angle of the room increased again.

"Hurry up, Cilla," Dad said. "This whole building feels like it's about to tip over."

Priscilla clambered further up the chair, stepping on the boy clone as she went.

"Ow!" Felicity yelped. "That hurts!"

Priscilla stretched her right leg forwards, placing her foot on the droid's base. She pushed down to make sure it would support her weight, then made a lunge for it. She landed with a thump, lying draped over the top of the droid like the saddle on a three-legged pony.

"Move forwards!" she ordered, and the droid jerked along, its feet clunking towards the exit door.

The flashing red light illuminated a button halfway up the door, set beside a keypad. Priscilla reached out and pushed the button. Nothing happened.

"I can't open it!" Priscilla called to no one in particular. "I need a pin code."

In response, the dog let out two short yaps.

"Two!" Dad called out.

The dog paused for several seconds, then: "Yip, yip, yip!"

Priscilla pressed three before Dad called it out this time.

"Yip, yip, yip, yip, yip, yip!"

"Two, three, six!" Dad called out, but the dog whined as Priscilla tried the handle. Still locked.

"Try it again, honey," Dad said to the dog.

Mum yapped twice, then instead of silence, she let out a whine.

"It's 2036!" Priscilla blurted out. "The year I was born."

She typed it into the keypad and the lights in the button turned from red to green.

"That's it!" Priscilla called out. "It's unlocked."

She slapped the button with her palm and the door hissed open.

Priscilla stared at the control room through the doorway. Mum had once showed her around some LMC control rooms on Earth, and those had been pretty impressive, but this was just ridiculous. There were thousands of buttons, levers and dials filling every inch of every wall. It was like fifty cockpits all squeezed into one.

As the droid carried her through the doorway, Priscilla felt a wave of panic. There was no way she'd be able to figure this out on her own.

"Droid... stop!" she said. D362 came to a halt on the other side of the doorway. If Priscilla leaned over she could still see the other clones strapped into their seats.

"Dad?" she called out in a shaky voice. "Can you come too?"

"Erm, yeah..." Dad's clone said. "But you'll have to send the robot back for me."

"Only authorised personnel can enter the control room," said the droid, and Priscilla's throat tightened. Would she have to figure this out all by herself?

"Who's authorised, then?" she asked, even though she was pretty sure she didn't want to know the answer.

"You, C7219 – Ella Freeman, and C8167 – Malcolm Freeman."

Priscilla glanced through the door at the body Dad was supposed to be in. He was leaning forwards as far as he could, sniffing at the air with his mouth open. There was a long string of dribble connecting his chin with his lap.

She was on her own.

As she had that thought, the door between the two rooms hissed shut. Priscilla was all alone in the control room.

The siren was not as loud in here. And the flashing red was accompanied by soft emergency lighting which illuminated all the screens and control panels.

Priscilla had no clue where to begin, but she was pretty sure that staying in the doorway would not help their situation. As if to prove the point, another tremor rattled the building and the angle of the room shifted again.

The droid swayed but its feet clung tight to the floor. For now. But how big an angle could it handle? Priscilla didn't want to find out. She had to stop it getting worse.

"Droid, take me to..." Priscilla said, her voice trailing off as she realised she didn't know where to go. But maybe the droid knew? "...the control panel that can fix this."

"Damage is critical. Approximately forty-two per cent of moon base is beyond repair."

That didn't sound good.

"What can I do, then? Should we just transmit straight back to Earth?"

"Negative. Transmission coordinates not aligned. Until moon base is stable, transmission is not possible."

That's just great, Priscilla thought. *We can't get out of here until this mess has been cleaned up. And me and Goliath are the only ones with the authority to do so. We're all going to die on this stupid rock!*

She looked around at all the screens and buttons, half of which displayed warning notifications.

All she wanted to do was close her eyes and wait for someone to come to her rescue. But that wasn't going to happen. She had to sort this out for herself.

She had to think.

Okay.

So, if forty-two per cent of the moon base was beyond repair, the whole family staying on Ganymede was probably not an option. It would be too dangerous.

But very soon their bodies back on Earth would be placed in stasis. Once that happened, going home wouldn't be an option, either.

Whatever she did, Priscilla had to do it quickly. If she could make the moon base stable, before their bodies were frozen, they could all go back to Earth.

"Droid, what's the best way to stabilise the moon base?"

"Analyse ground stability. Disconnect nonessential modules to stabilise core areas."

Priscilla rubbed her face with her hands. Why did the droid have to make everything sound so complicated?

"Take me to the control panel where I can analyse the ground stability."

The droid lurched forwards under Priscilla's weight. As it turned she had to shift her body around to the upwards side of the slope to avoid slipping off. It took several minutes for the droid to battle the gradient and arrive at an enormous control panel with more red lights than green.

The readout screen displayed random numbers and symbols. There were a few diagrams of different parts of the moon base, but Priscilla felt like she was looking at one of Dad's cryptic crosswords. None of it made any sense.

Since the droid had proved itself useful so far, Priscilla tried her luck again.

"D362, could you please summarise the information for me?"

The droid's head rose a few inches, and because Priscilla was draped over it, she moved upwards too. Its red eyes stared at the screen for several seconds before it responded.

"Instability caused by fissures underneath the western wing. The weight of overlying modules is destabilising core areas."

"Which modules need to be released?"

The whole room lurched as the droid's eyes scanned the screen again. It felt like they were slipping down a hole.

"Quickly!" Priscilla added.

"The Garden Pod is causing eighty-seven percent of the downward pull. Releasing that should provide sufficient stability."

That's typical, thought Priscilla. *The one thing on this stupid rock that makes life bearable, and I need to drop it into a fissure!*

"How do I release it?" Priscilla asked, staring at the screen filled with gobbledygook.

"Select P947, then press the red *Disconnect* button."

Priscilla scanned the screen. Eventually she saw an elevated segment of the moon base labelled P947. She tapped that section and it became highlighted in green. Now all she needed to do was find the *Disconnect* button. The problem was that there were about four million buttons to choose from, and three million of them were red.

She spotted a large button to the top right of the screen that had *Disconnect* through its middle.

She held her hand above the button, but paused. Was this really the right thing to do? Was this what her Mum would have done? She wanted to rush back out to the other room and ask her. One bark for yes, two barks for no. But she didn't have time. The room felt like it was balancing on the edge of a precipice, and judging by the information on the screen, it probably was.

Without giving it another thought, Priscilla jabbed her index finger at the button.

Eight dashes appeared on the screen, above the words *Authorisation Code Required.*

Blast it! Why did it have to be an eight-digit PIN number? Couldn't the authorisation code be the same as the door code?

Priscilla's first thought was to get her mum to bark out the new code. But the room was swaying like a tree in a breeze. She had to figure this out for herself.

How many digits was their home phone number? Priscilla counted it out on her hand. Nine digits. No good.

Hang on. If she'd used the year that Priscilla was born for the door code, then Mum might have used her entire date of birth for the authorisation code. She typed 04022036 into the keypad.

"Authorisation denied!"

Come on. Think! Okay, so she used my birth year for the door code. But I'm not her only daughter. Maybe she used Felicity's birth year as well? When was Felicity born?

Priscilla wracked her brains for a moment, then typed 20362041 into the keypad.

"Authorisation denied!"

"Think, you idiot, think!" she said aloud, as the room tilted even further.

"What should I think about?" the droid replied.

"No, not you!"

She rubbed her face with one hand. The other was gripping the droid to stop her from joining all the furniture at the bottom end of the room.

If it wasn't the years, maybe it was a combination of the days and months of their birthdays. It was worth a try, and Priscilla couldn't think of anything else. If this didn't work they'd have to go and ask Mum to bark it out. But judging by how badly the control room was swaying, Priscilla didn't think there'd be enough time for that.

She typed 04022407 into the keypad.

There was a pause of several seconds, in which Priscilla could hear her own heartbeat, even over the distant siren.

"Authorised!" flashed up on the screen in big letters.

There was a loud click in the distance, like a gun going off. Then the floor dropped away from beneath Priscilla's feet.

She gripped the droid's arm to stop herself being left behind in mid-air. Her stomach lurched, like on a roller coaster, as she followed the droid downward, panic filling her chest.

The panic was replaced with pain as her body crashed down on top of the droid. There was a deafening boom as the moon base hit the ground. The objects that had piled up on the lower side of the room were catapulted up into the air and came raining down all around her. A fire extinguisher smashed the screen next to her, then bounced along the wall, destroying levers and buttons as it went. A chair spun by, whooshing past her head.

Priscilla yelped but kept hugging the droid, which was now beside her, its arms stretched out wide. She flinched as a metal box glanced off the droid's hand and ricocheted off into the corner. It had been heading directly for her face!

The siren still wailed in the distance, but compared to the crash of the moon base and the downpour of furniture, it was quiet and calming.

Priscilla looked up from her shelter beside the droid. The control room was almost level now, but there was debris everywhere and several of the screens were smashed. Those that still worked were flickering with warning messages.

She couldn't believe she was okay. The droid had saved her life. Its feet had kept it from being flung around, and it had stretched its arms over her head to protect her.

"Thank you, D362," she said, her voice sounding hollow and shaky. "You saved my life."

The droid didn't respond.

Priscilla ducked out from underneath its arms and walked around to its other side. A chair had landed on top of D362, its leg smashing straight through the droid's face screen. An intricate web of cracks surrounded the hole and all its lights had gone out, leaving no sign of life at all.

She kissed her hand and tapped it on top of the droid's head, then turned to face the door to the transmission room.

Her family!

Priscilla dashed towards the door, panic clawing its way up her throat. If a chair had done that to the droid, what was she going to find on the other side of that door?

Were her family okay?

She quickly punched her birth year into the keypad and hit the lock. The door hissed open and Priscilla rushed through.

"Oh, thank goodness you're okay!" the young female clone – her dad – said. "How on earth did you survive that crash without being strapped in?"

"The droid, D362," she panted. "It saved my life!" She stared around the transmission room. There was debris all over the floor, but it wasn't as bad as the chaos in the control room. And her family were all okay. The young male clone – Felicity – had his arm outstretched and was holding Dad's hand. The small dog was still in its box, staring up at Priscilla.

Even Goliath was okay in the male clone's body. Although there was a dark patch on the front of his trousers.

"How come we're still alive?" Dad asked. "It felt like we just fell off a cliff!"

"No, that was me releasing the Garden Pod to stabilise the moon base. But there's so much damage... I don't think we can stay here."

Dad turned the clone's head to one side and stared at Priscilla. It was hard to read the expression on that strange pale face. Was it pride? Or annoyance at her not wanting to be here?

"It would also be nice to get us all in the right bodies," she added. "So... maybe we transmit back to Earth?"

The dog yapped and gave what looked like a double thumbs-up.

"But how are we going to do that without your mother's help?"

Priscilla looked at the command panel next to the transmission tower. The screens were all intact, and it looked way less complicated than the control room.

"I'll see if I can figure it out," Priscilla said, stepping up to the screen.

She wished D362 was here to help her,

but suddenly felt like perhaps she didn't need help.

She looked at the screen, scanning the readouts from the previous transmission. All of the information was okay, except for a big red box saying *Connection Lost*.

She tapped the button marked *Re-establish Connection* and hit *Go*.

The loading icon spun around for several seconds, then the box turned green.

"I think I've got it," she said out loud. "I've connected with the transmission tower on Earth."

She found a button that said *Reverse Previous Transmission* and tapped it. The loading symbol flashed up for several more seconds, until the screen filled with diagrams showing their minds being transmitted from each of the clones, back into their original bodies. She checked that everyone was going to the correct places and turned to face her family.

"I've done it!" she said, a smile breaking out on her face. "We're going home."

Priscilla hit the *Commence Countdown* button and rushed back to her seat. By the time she had fumbled with her safety belt the countdown had already got to six.

"FIVE, FOUR, THREE..."

She reached out and held Felicity's other hand, flashing her a smile.

"TWO, ONE... TRANSMIT!"

She glanced up at the control screen to check that there were no warning signs, as her chair vibrated.

The thrum filled her ears, drowning out the wailing that had been the constant soundtrack during their brief stay on Ganymede.

Priscilla kept her eyes open, but everything faded away.

This time she enjoyed the nothingness. No sirens. No aches and pains. No worry. Just a calm stretch of being, as her mind whizzed across the solar system.

Then all her senses engaged at once. Deep vibrations filled her ears again. Her body shuddered and shook. The bright LED lighting forced her to squint and cover her eyes with her hand.

And it actually was *her* hand... she could see that instantly. Her dark skin. The familiar freckles. Her recently chewed fingernails.

Priscilla was back in her own body!

Mum had already unbuckled her safety belt and was barking instructions at the viewing window.

"Get Ganesh Singh back up here NOW!" she yelled. "And I need complete stats on the moon-base damage. ASAP."

Her mum was definitely back. She patted down her body as she turned to face her family. "Well... *that* was a total disaster. Is everyone okay? Are we all back in the correct bodies?"

Priscilla nodded, turning to check that her father and sister were also nodding.

Goliath's huge frame was still squeezed into the glass container and he was busy licking his own paw. He looked happy to be back, too.

Mum ran her fingers through her hair. "That was not an enjoyable experience, was it?"

"I don't know," Dad said, "it was nice to feel so young again. And I enjoyed watching Priscilla do all the hard work."

Mum smiled at Priscilla for a moment. "I'm very proud of you, honey. You were so brave and responsible." Then she glanced at her watch. "Even if we were only gone for an hour and seventeen minutes, rather than three years."

Priscilla looked down at the floor. She wasn't thinking about her actions on the moon base. She'd had to do that. There had been no other way. She was feeling bad about how she'd behaved before they left. She'd been so childish.

Suddenly Priscilla could see things from her mum's perspective. She'd had to make a difficult decision. For her career. For her family. And Priscilla had made it even harder.

"I'm sorry, Mum," she said. "I shouldn't have behaved like that beforehand. I know it was a tough decision for you."

"Well, I can see why you were worried. If I'd known I'd be putting you all in so much danger, I never would have agreed to it," Mum said. "We certainly won't be doing that again."

A heavy weight settled in Priscilla's stomach.

Maybe living on Ganymede wouldn't be so bad, after all. It would bring them closer together as a family. And perhaps Mum would teach her what all those buttons and leavers did. Suddenly, engineering didn't seem like the boring job she'd always thought it was.

"Why don't we wait until they've repaired the base and then give it another go?" Priscilla suggested.

Mum tilted her head to the side and smiled.

She didn't have time to answer, though. The team of technicians rushed into the room. Most of them started unfastening straps, but an important-looking lady stopped and waited to speak to Mum.

"I think that is a decision we need to make together," Mum said. "As a family. But right now, I've got to work hard to get things back on track. I look forward to talking – and listening – to you later."

Mum squeezed Priscilla's hand, then turned and spoke to the technician.

"Come on, kids," Dad said. "Let's relocate to the food table. There might still be some eclairs left."

ALSO BY TOM E. MOFFATT

FREE EBOOK

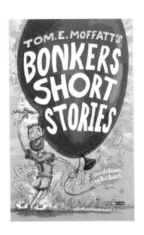

If you want to be in a draw to win TEN SQUILLION DOLLARS following the link below will not help you. However, if you'd like to receive an original short story by Tom E. Moffatt, as well as sample stories from the first three Bonkers Collections, then going to www.TomEMoffatt.com/books is a very good idea. You'll also receive occasional emails to let you know when Tom E. Moffatt has a new book coming out. And if you're really unlucky, he might tell you a joke or two…

www.TomEMoffatt.com/books

BONKERS SHORT STORIES
VOLUMES 1 & 2

MIND-SWAPPING MADNESS

A boy in a fly's body. A toad waiting to be kissed. Horses that know Morse code and aliens who hijack children's bodies. Has everyone gone completely bonkers?

These hilarious, action-packed stories transport you to a world where mind-swapping is possible. But be warned: looking in the mirror will never be the same again.

BODY-HOPPING HYSTERICS

Not all superpowers are a good thing. Especially NOT if your mum has them. Or if they're fuelled by embarrassment. And what if you can't find your way back home?

Jump out of your skin with these hilarious short stories by award-winning author, Tom E. Moffatt. But don't leave your body unattended for long!

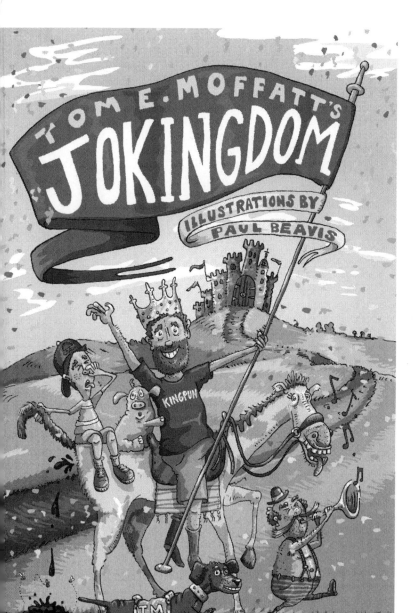

TOM E. MOFFATT'S
JOKINGDOM

ILLUSTRATIONS BY
PAUL BEAVIS

TOM E. MOFFATT'S JOKINGDOM

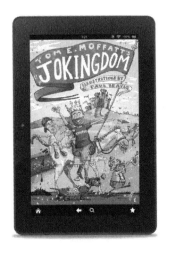

I'm joking. You're joking. Everyone's joking in Tom E. Moffatt's Jokingdom.

Laugh your socks off with thousands of original jokes, improve your delivery skills and even have a crack at creating your own hilarious howlers.

From a FREE ebook to full-length paperbacks crammed with jokes, instructions, and practice exercises, explore Tom E. Moffatt's Jokingdom now and become the funniest joker in the land.

www.TomEMoffatt.com/jokingdom

ABOUT THE AUTHOR

Tom E. Moffatt likes to MIX UP his writing projects. Some days he works on his Bonkers short stories, sometimes he writes jokes or chapter books. At other times he slams the lid of his laptop shut and heads to the beach with his wife and three daughters. But whatever he chooses to do that day, MAYHEM is almost guaranteed.

For more silliness, jokes and information go to
www.TomEMoffatt.com

You're still here?

That can't be a mix-up. You must really love this book! If that is the case, please do me a favour: tell other people all about *Mix-up Mayhem*. I'm always looking for new readers and word-of-mouth is one of the best ways to find them.

Or if you want to tell thousands of people all at once, perhaps you could leave a review on your favourite online store? It doesn't have to be anything fancy... just a few words to let people know what to expect. It also lets me know what works and what doesn't, so I can keep writing the kinds of books that you want to read.

Printed in Great Britain
by Amazon